Christy

MAUD
JOHNSON

SCHOLASTIC BOOK SERVICES
New York Toronto London Auckland Sydney Tokyo

ISBN 0-590-31261-8

Copyright © 1979 by Maud Johnson. All rights reserved. Published by Scholastic Book Services, a Division of Scholastic Magazines, Inc.

12 11 10 9 8 7 6 5 4 3 2   0 1 2 3 4/8

Christy

A Wildfire Book

Chapter

· 1 ·

The first time I ever saw *him* was at the Greenview Service Station on a cold, murky January afternoon when the clouds looked as if snow was on its way and the air was sharp enough to make my skin tingle. My mother and I had been buying groceries and the backseat of our car was loaded with brown paper bags of food while I sat in front beside Mama, the egg cartons on my lap as a safety precaution.

We were on our way to the house. It was too early for me to think of that unfamiliar building as home — eventually I would, of course, but not yet. Glancing at the gasoline gauge, Mama commented that she'd better have the tank filled, and as we were new in the area she had to drive around looking for a gas station.

1

"There's a place," I said three or four blocks later, gesturing past a shoe repair shop and a bakery to the red and white sign which proclaimed: GREENVIEW SERVICE STATION — GAS, OIL, REPAIRS.

She braked at the gas pumps and a middle-aged man came to the car, nodding when she told him what she wanted. A tall, lanky boy who seemed to be about my age or slightly older also appeared and began to clean the windshield. He started on the driver's side, squirting liquid from a plastic bottle onto the glass and wiping it off with several thicknesses of blue paper, polishing the surface in small, overlapping strokes.

He was bundled up against the cold in a heavy khaki jacket and a black knitted cap which covered his ears, and those circular motions he made must have hypnotized me after a fashion because I realized I was staring at him. It wasn't that he was spectacularly handsome, although there was something rather attractive about his triangular-shaped face. His eyes were blue under dark eyebrows which matched the brown hair showing beneath the edge of the knitted cap and the icy wind had put dabs of ruddy color on his cheekbones. The hand shining the windshield was large and raw-boned, the knuckles chapped.

As soon as he finished the driver's side, he came around the end of the car to work on the glass in front of me. Our eyes met through the windshield and I was embarrassed to be caught watching him so intently;

2

my face was hot enough all of a sudden to let me know I must be blushing. Maybe he realized I was flustered and wanted to put me at ease or maybe he was naturally friendly, because he grinned and said, "Hi, there."

He had to be speaking to me. My mother was talking with the middle-aged man and there was nobody else in sight.

"Hi," I answered and rolled down my window. A blast of cold air surged into the automobile.

"Are you folks tourists just passing through?" he asked, his arm moving a steady rhythm as he made fresh circles on the glass. "I saw the New York State license tags on your car. We get a few tourists in hot weather but not many this time of year."

"We've moved here," I said. "Yesterday."

"No kidding? How'd you happen to choose Virginia? Especially Greenview?"

"My father was transferred here. He's going to manage the Crenshaw Company."

"Oh — you mean the electric motor plant?" The boy's eyebrows went up. "I thought Mr. Harlow was boss there."

"He used to be," I explained. "But he's been sent to the West Coast and Dad is taking over here."

The boy stopped wiping long enough to refold the wad of blue paper, apparently searching for a dry spot on it. I thought he had finished chatting with me but I was wrong.

"Where will you be living?" he asked.

"Dad bought the Harlows' house. It's a couple of miles out of town."

"Sure. I know the one. Part of the old Toscin farm." He gave a mischievous grin. "It's the house with all those crazy windows."

His description made me smile as the house had nine bay windows. I'd counted them the previous day when we arrived, dumbfounded at the odd architecture of the hilltop building which would be my new home.

The boy continued to polish the car's gleaming windshield. Finally he stopped so that his face was on the level with mine by the open window and despite the several inches of space separating us, his breath felt warm against my cheek. I knew I must be blushing again.

"Will you go to Greenview High?" he asked.

I murmured yes and he smiled once more. He had the whitest teeth I'd ever seen.

"Then I'll see you at school," he added. "I go there, too."

I tried to think of something to say, something bright and intelligent and friendly to let him know I hoped to see him again and that I wasn't a clod. But my mind went blank. He waited a long minute, his eyes on my face, and when I remained silent he straightened up, his smile vanishing. He had expected me to keep the conversation going. I was aware of it and hated myself for not being able to talk to a boy with ease unless

I knew him very, very well, and even then it was hard.

My mother paid for the gasoline and closed her purse. Glancing toward me, she reached for the ignition switch and said, "Ready, Christy?" What she wanted to know was if I'd finished talking to the boy. I hadn't, but it was obvious he was through with me.

My, "Yes," got caught in my throat and I nodded. As she pulled the car out into the street I looked back to see the boy drop his wad of wet blue paper into the trash can next to the gas pumps and quickly jam his hands into the pockets of his jacket. He was striding toward the service station office with long steps, his shoulders hunched up almost to his ears as if he was half-frozen.

I could have asked him questions about school, I thought, furious with myself. I could have told him my name . . . and he undoubtedly would have mentioned his. He looked nice and he seemed friendly. His smile was wonderful.

If only I hadn't acted so stupidly. . . .

way to the house that afternoon, I was still
thinking about the boy, wishing I'd behaved
differently, and she must have had her mind
on something.

Chapter

· 2 ·

My mother and I talked very little on the way to the house that afternoon. I was still thinking about the boy, wishing I'd behaved differently, and she must have had her mind on something.

The January darkness was swooping down quickly, even though it was just a few minutes after five o'clock. Not much traffic moved in our direction, and as we passed the town limits sign and were away from houses and streetlamps, the car's headlights put pale yellow smudges on the pavement in front of us. Snow began to spatter on the windshield which the boy at the service station had cleaned so vigorously, the flakes melting as soon as they touched the glass and leaving tiny globs of water which trickled an inch or two. I had the feeling we were caught under a mammoth gray bowl turned upside down. The sky was the color of unpolished pewter and the Blue Ridge Mountains which rimmed the landscape were no longer blue, but an ominous gray-black.

Twilight can be a lonesome time of day. For me, at least. A lump rose into my throat and the hollow ache inside of me made my ribs feel taut as if they were squeezing my heart and lungs, making every breath a hurt. I recognized the painful sensation: homesickness. And I knew there wasn't much to be done about it until enough time had gone by to let it disappear of its own accord.

The terrible part was that at the moment my family had no real home. Putting our belongings into a strange house in Virginia didn't turn it instantly into a familiar spot. Everything might be neat and clean, even beautiful, but that wouldn't make it "home" any more than a motel room became home just because my clothes hung in the closet or my toothbrush was in the bathroom.

Dad had been transferred so many times I was well aware of all the hurting symptoms of homesickness. It wasn't that I thought New York, where we'd been living, was the greatest or that I longed to spend the rest of my life there. I didn't, but I knew my way around the school and the town we'd just left. I had learned what to expect from those people. There were teenagers in that community who, at last, were including me in their parties and fun.

Now, I would need to start all over again.

The various places we lived when I was small were a blur in my mind and moving then was endurable so long as I had Mama and Dad, my bicycle, and the Raggedy Ann doll and pink stuffed bunny which were my sleep companions. Now that I'd reached the middle teens, though, pulling up roots was a nightmare. I'd started Junior High in Michigan. A year later Dad was transferred to Texas, and after that, to New York. The latest transfer put us in Virginia.

From experience I could guess what lay ahead. The next several weeks — maybe months — would be grim. I wasn't naturally pessimistic but I knew it would take time to feel contented in a new place. Going to a new high school was agony and the same was true of trying to make new friends when I was a stranger and the other students had been acquainted most of their lives. I'd have to smile often; sometimes I'd have to smile when I felt like sobbing. I'd be stared at, sized up, whispered about, all of which I must ignore as if I didn't realize it was happening. For an endless time I'd be on the outside of school activities and clubs, watching the others my age, the ones I longed to be friends with, hoping desperately to be included, but not daring to push myself into the various groups because that was a sure way to be disliked. It was necessary to wait until they wanted me.

Some girls who weren't wary of a newcomer, I had discovered the hard way in the past, were the ones who didn't have a friend to their names. Boys were less wary, or maybe they didn't resent a new girl the way they would a new fellow, or maybe their curiosity got the better of them. But boys liked girls who were sexy — and I wasn't — and boys didn't go wild over a girl who was strictly average.

A mental picture of myself went through my mind as though I was seeing my reflection in a full-length mirror. Average figure. Average looking brown hair. Hazel eyes. Straight teeth from years of wearing braces, although my teeth weren't as even and dazzlingly white as those of the boy at the service station.

I hadn't wanted to move to Virginia. To move any place, for that matter. We'd only lived in New York eighteen months and I was halfway into my junior year of high school — expecting, hoping we would stay where we were until I graduated, but two days after Christmas Dad had broken the news about our forthcoming move.

I'd just come in from ice skating that December afternoon, having a marvelous time at a frozen lake with a crowd from my class at school, and at dusk the western sky was still rosy from the last remnants of a sparkling, sunshiny day. Opening our front door, I got a whiff of meat loaf, one of my favorites.

"That you, Christy?" Mama called from the back of the house.

My mother always asked that same question when she was expecting me home. A soft metallic sound, the clinking together of knives, forks, and spoons, let me know she was setting the table for dinner.

"I'll be there to help as soon as I put my skates away. Everything smells great," I answered and went through the living room and down the corridor.

My bedroom was on one side of the hall opposite my parents' room. Their door stood open with the overhead light on and I paused, the skates in one hand and my scarf and mittens in the other, eyeing the suitcase spread open on the bed. Dad, his back toward me, was taking shirts and underwear out of the bureau, counting the garments methodically which was his way of making sure he'd have enough clean clothes for however long he was to be out of town. I had seen him do that a hundred times.

"Are we going someplace?" I asked.

Both my parents originally came from Indiana. We visited there each summer and occasionally went to see relatives in winter, during school vacations.

"I have a business trip to Virginia," he answered. "We're eating dinner early tonight so you and your mother can drive me to the airport."

"A *business* trip between Christmas and New Year's?" That struck me as odd. The plant where my father was assistant manager had been closed since Christmas Eve to give the employees a holiday. It wasn't scheduled to reopen until the second of January.

Dad began taking socks from another bureau drawer, counting them just as he counted the other garments. My mother always rolled a pair of clean socks into a ball, and Dad had five of those small, dark bundles in his hands. He would be gone five days — or four, with an extra day's clothing in case he needed it.

"Christy, I may as well let you know now," he said. "I've had a promotion and we'll be moving to Virgina in January."

"Moving?" The word tore from me in a ragged gasp. "Oh, no! No!"

Dad's head jerked, his eyes widening. My mother must have heard what we were saying because she ran out of the kitchen and down the corridor to join us. A streak of flour made a white smear across her green-flowered apron.

"I know how you feel about moving, Christy." Dad's voice was hoarse and it hadn't been that way moments earlier. "When we came here I told my boss you were in senior high and that I didn't want you to have to change schools again before you graduate, but this opening in Virginia is the kind of opportunity I can't turn down."

"Bryan will be manager of the Virginia plant. In complete charge," Mama chimed in. "It's an honor for him and proof that the head officials in the company recognize his ability because the other plant managers in the firm are much older."

I glanced from one of my parents to the other, seeing the two vertical frown lines between my father's eyebrows and the way Mama's jaw was tightening, a sure sign she was tense. She and Dad didn't appear happy. Dad's promotion might be fantastic but either they didn't want to move any more than I did or they were disturbed by my reaction. We were close, the three of us. Maybe it's often like that in small families. Dad and Mama were my friends as well as my parents.

"C-Couldn't we — we wait until June when school is — is out?" I asked shakily.

Dad came to me and patted my shoulder. "I'm afraid not, Christy," he said. "There's a messy situation at the Virgina plant and I'm needed there as soon as possible."

"You mean we're moving *now*?" A rock seemed to be pressing on my chest, making it hard for me to breathe.

"No, I'm going tonight, to look the situation over and find us a place to live. I'll be back shortly to wind up everything in this area and head south again, and you and your mother will stay on here through your midterm exams."

My classes would start again the second day of January, the same time the local plant reopened. Mid-terms were scheduled to start ten days later. That meant in less than three weeks we would be leaving for Virginia. I shuddered involuntarily.

"Christy, I hope — " my father began and he sounded desperate.

"Wait, Bryan," Mama interrupted. "Christy isn't a child and you don't have to make excuses for accepting the promotion. She understands that the company you work for transfers its key personnel a lot and I'm sure she'll adjust to a new area just as you and I will adjust and just as she's adjusted to all the other places we've lived. A girl as pretty and sweet and smart as she is can handle this sort of situation."

Pretty . . . sweet . . . smart . . . Mama was trying to bolster my morale. She probably believed I was all of those things since mothers have a way of thinking differently from other people where their own children are concerned.

At the moment I didn't feel pretty or sweet or smart. I just felt pitiful, and because I was scared to death I was going to burst into tears, I mumbled something and ran to my room, closing the door behind me.

On the thirty-mile drive back home after leaving the airport that night, my mother mentioned the move. I'd had very little to say during dinner or afterward while Mama and Dad kept up a conversation which seemed forced, as if neither of them could stand to be silent. Dad's hug was unusually hard when he got out of the car at the entrance to the terminal building. My mother, who had been beside him in front, slid under the steering wheel and I came from the backseat to sit beside her. I had my driver's license and if things had been different, I probably would have asked to drive home, but that night there was too much on my mind for me to be able to concentrate on traffic.

The sky was clear and starry. The highway had been swept clean of snow and the dark pavement glistened under the glare of our headlights, while land bordering the road gleamed with a pale icy crust.

Mama stretched one hand toward the radio knob on the dashboard but must have changed her mind about wanting to listen to music or a news program as she promptly returned her hand to the steering wheel. "Christy, I know how you feel about moving," she sighed. "And so does your father."

Everything bottled up inside of me exploded. "Oh, no you don't!" I blurted out. "You couldn't! It's easy for you! You don't have to walk into a school where you don't know one living soul and have all the students stare at you! You couldn't possibly understand!"

There was the barest whisper of sound as she sucked her breath in. "I can imagine how it must be for you," she said. "I have to go into a community where I don't know anyone but you and Bryan and I have to find a doctor for us and a dentist and find a church and a good grocery store and hope to make friends. I also have to try to turn a strange house into a home. It isn't easy for me, either."

"Then why did you agree to move?" Bitterness echoed in my voice. "If you told Dad you didn't want to go, he'd stay where we are even if the move does mean a promotion."

She passed a slow-moving car before replying. At first I thought she was deliberately ignoring my question, but it wasn't that way. "My life is wrapped up in you and Bryan," she said at last, speaking so softly I had to strain to catch every word. "Making a home is my career. Oh, someday if we're in one town long enough for me to feel settled, maybe I'll get a job. I believe that when a man is a marvelous husband and father it's up to his family to live wherever his work takes him unless there's a good reason not to do it."

Ahead of us was a huge truck with a row of red lights across the tailgate and one of the lights, the second from the left, was dimmer than the others. I found my eyes glued to it and because I didn't know what to say, I kept silent.

"Bryan told me the day he started with this company that we were in for several moves but it's all a means to an end," Mama went on, her voice stronger now. "Apparently he's been singled out for a bright future since he's being given such diversified experience now, and if he can turn things around at the Virginia plant it'll be a feather in his cap."

"Turn things around?" I repeated, puzzled. "What do you mean?"

"The last manager there must have been a disaster. The Virginia plant couldn't meet production schedules and lost money. Bryan says Mr. Harlow — Ira Harlow was the previous manager — is a brilliant person but he must not know how to deal with people as the employees were dissatisfied and he even antagonized some of the people in the community. So did his wife, according to what Bryan has learned. Heavens!" My mother gave a choppy laugh. "I thought all company wives learned in a hurry how to smile and grit their teeth and keep their opinions to themselves. Even if they hate it."

"Is Mr. Harlow still at the Virginia plant?" I asked.

"No. He's already been transferred to the West Coast. Demoted, your father said. The plant is without a manager and that's why Bryan is needed in such a hurry. Listen to me, Christy!" She dropped the confidential tone and became stern. "You're not to mention one bit of this when we get to Virginia! Do you understand that? I've probably told you more than I should have."

I nodded in the darkness. For a few minutes my mother had talked to me as one adult to another, but now that she was ordering me not to repeat our conversation, she sounded as if she thought I was in kindergarten. Strangely enough, in a way that's how I felt. Grown sometimes, and at other moments, scared and ill at ease, especially around strangers.

"What's the name of our town?" I asked.

"Greenview."

"Is it near the ocean?"

"No, it's in the west-central part of the state rather than on the coast. Rolling land bordered by the Blue Ridge Mountains and

Bryan said it's supposed to be a beautiful area."

I hoped aloud that Greenview was a city, thinking there would be more to do in a large place with fabulous stores, museums, and restaurants than in a small town. Also, a city would give me a choice of schools.

"I'm afraid Greenview is rather small, Christy," my mother explained. "About five thousand inhabitants. Five thousand and three after we come."

If that last remark was meant to be funny, the humor passed over my head. "Oh, brother," I groaned. "That means one high school and all the students will have known each other since they were born. They'll make me feel like I'm a freak. Mama, can't you and I stay on here until school closes in June? Please! That would give me the chance to get to know some of the teenagers in Greenview during the summer and I wouldn't be a total stranger when school opens in the fall."

She shook her head. "It really isn't possible, dear."

"Why not? Why isn't it possible?"

"If this were April or May, you and I could wait in New York until June, but the school year is only half gone. Besides, Bryan wants us with him and I can't bear to be away from him for such a long time or to think of his going home every night to a silent house or having to stay in a motel for months. He hates that sort of living. With so much of the school year remaining before summer vacation, we'll leave when you finish your midterm exams."

My mother's profile was silhouetted against the lights of the oncoming cars, her chin lifted so that I saw the graceful curve of her throat. I'd always thought she was beautiful with her oval face and slightly turned up nose. My nose turned up a little, too, but it didn't look as attractive to me as hers.

It hadn't occurred to me before that she would dread moving. Like me, she would be new in a strange place and perhaps she would have to fight homesickness, aching for familiar friends and surroundings as much as I would. Moving could be hard on Dad, too, something I hadn't considered until that moment. Each new job was a promotion and undoubtedly a challenge to him, but that did not mean he relished pulling up stakes so often.

It's a shock to peer into another person's heart. Suddenly, I was almost embarrassed at what I was discovering about Mama. Taking my eyes from her profile, I focused on the white line painted down the center of the highway. The road was straight and the line stretched ahead as far as I could see. My hands were clasped together in my lap. I was thinking how cruel it would be to my parents for me to moan endlessly about the moving and the inevitable loneliness. Griping and complaining wouldn't help me and it would upset Mama and Dad.

I'd try to make myself satisfied in Virgina,

I decided silently, no matter how difficult it might be. Another thought tumbled through my mind, a wistful one. If only I could find a friend quickly in this new place, a girl to enjoy being with, somebody to phone, to pal around with at school . . . Maybe — just maybe — there would be a boy in the high school at Greenview who wasn't already going steady and who would want to date me. . . .

It was a dream and I knew it. Wishful thinking on my part. Still, it didn't hurt to hope.

Chapter

· 3 ·

Dad returned to New York from Virginia and hurried south again shortly after New Year's Day while my mother and I drove down two weeks later.

Unusual was the most fitting word I could think of to describe our new home. Actually it was only new to us as the house had been built in the early 1900's and Dad bought it from the Harlows who seemed eager to be rid of all ties with Virginia.

"I hate to buy a house without your seeing it first, Susan," Dad told Mama on the telephone. "But the real estate agent says other prospective buyers are looking at the place."

Mama and I had been doing the dinner dishes when Dad called, and when she hung up she told me some of the things he'd said. The house had big rooms with high ceilings, there were several fireplaces although it had a furnace, and the view was magnificent. The living room, dining room, a small den, and big eat-in kitchen were on the ground floor, with three bedrooms upstairs.

"Bryan says two acres of land come with it," she went on. "Plenty of space for a nice garden." Her eyes lit up. My mother loved to grow things and no matter how small our yards were previously, she always raised flowers.

Mama tried to prepare me for something different at our new home in Virginia, something unlike the modern apartments and split levels where we lived in the past, but I must have been too engrossed in studying for exams to pay a great deal of attention. That was why, on the first day in Greenview, I was surprised at the tall, skinny house, white with dark green trim, set in a grove of trees on the very top of a hill. In the back there was a sunny flat area at the bottom of the hill, the place for the garden. We were in the country, not in town, for there wasn't another house in sight, and my eyes were riveted to the place we would live.

Bright sunshine glinted off the dark roof and fresh white paint of a house which was neither beautiful nor ugly, just very unusual. If I'd seen that house in a movie I would have been sure there was a ghost in the attic or that it was the home of a strange little old lady in black silk who served poisoned tea in dainty bone china cups. The building appeared oddly out of proportion, too tall for its narrow width, which made it look as though a hard wind could topple it into the valley below. Then I remembered how long it had been standing on the hill, since the early 1900's. As Dad pointed out, the house was intended to last.

A narrow porch went across the front with double doors made out of mellowed brown oak leading inside. Around the peaked roof just under the eaves was an elaborate dark green wooden molding of spirals and curliques which my mother called "gingerbread."

She shaded her eyes with one hand against the sun as she tilted her head up to stare at the roof. "Did you ever see so many bay windows?"

I, too, was looking at the windows. I had seen bays before, three-sided windows projecting out from the walls, but not more than one or two on a single house, and this building had three bay windows on the front. Two flanked the entrance with a third above the door on the second story, and more bays were visible on the side. I got out of the car, my feet crunching on the stubble of wintry brown grass as I circled the house to count the bays. There were nine in all.

Dad fell into step with me as I neared the car again. Mama was already inside the house.

"Amazing windows, aren't they?" he said and smiled, making it more of a statement than a question.

"There's even a bay window in the back," I reported.

"It seems the Mr. Toscin, who built this house, installed the bays so that no matter which room he was in, there would be a broad view of the mountains." Dad lifted his arm to make a sweeping gesture toward the landscape behind us. "You'll have to admit the scenery from this hill is spectacular, Christy."

My eyes slid along the horizon where five ranges of mountains bordered the cloudless sky. One range rose behind the next, all of them rounded on top rather than with a contour of jagged peaks, and the range nearest to us was a rich, smoky blue with each row of mountains behind it looming slightly paler until the final one was a misty blue line in the distance. Between those mountains and our hill lay the highway and rolling pastureland where scattered fences marked boundaries. A flock of sheep grazed in one section and a herd of jet-black cattle stood near a small pond, the reflection of the sky turning the pond water a vivid blue. The animals were in a cluster except for one cow which stood a short way apart facing the others.

Dad turned from the mountains to look at me. "You didn't say how you like it, Christy."

I almost answered, "It's okay but . . . ," not knowing what to utter after the *but*. And I couldn't pretend that it was. I swallowed hard. It was necessary for me to say something because my father's eyes were boring into my face. He wanted very much for me to like our new-old house and the hilltop and the scenery. I was as sure of it as if he'd shouted the fact.

"It's super," I managed to say, and my throat felt uncommonly dry from the fib. I didn't sound convincing to myself but Dad seemed instantly relieved.

There is no explanation for what I said next. The words weren't meant to be as critical as they sounded and I didn't want any more discussion about the move or the house with nine bay windows or my opinion of the town of Greenview. Somehow, though, my mouth burned with sentences which were caught behind my tongue waiting to come out.

"Why didn't you warn me we have to live out in the country?" I demanded, a fierce accusation in my tone. "I should have thought at least we'd be in town. Near people. I didn't think we'd have to be isolated out here in the sticks without any neighbors or — or — " My voice froze at the consternation washing over his features.

"Dad, I don't mean — I'm not blaming you or — or anything," I floundered. "It's just different from what I expected. More — uh — rural than where we've lived before."

"This isn't way out in the sticks, Christy. We're only a couple of miles from town and transportation won't be a problem for you since the school bus stops at the bottom of our hill. Your mother will have her car and you can use that when you need it. Shall we see what Susan is doing inside?"

I was thankful he'd changed the subject, and we walked up the broad wooden steps and into a narrow hall with a curving stair to join Mama.

"Incidentally, Christy," Dad said as he closed the front doors behind us, "I notified the high school that you'll report for classes on Monday. With tomorrow being Friday, it's pointless for you to rush to enroll this close to the weekend. The principal is John Brady and he seemed quite anxious to be cooperative. I told him your records were being mailed from your last school."

Monday. The word rang in my ears. Monday would be my private D-Day, the time my ordeal started in earnest. I liked school and making passing grades had never been a problem for me, but on Monday I'd have to steel myself to tolerate the whispers and inquisitive stares or, what could be worse, the isolation of being completely ignored. Either way, it was guaranteed to be a rough experience. I'd changed schools often enough to know.

My personal thoughts were interrupted by the sound of the moving van with our belongings chugging up the hill, and for the remainder of that Thursday and half of the next day I stayed busy helping to get the house straight. My mother claimed that one thing she knew how to do expertly was to move, which was correct.

In contrast to Thursday's clear sky and sunshine, Friday was overcast with a sharp wind whipping the tree branches back and forth and heavy dark clouds banked low on the horizon. "Snow clouds," Mama said. The mountains were a different gray, not blue as I'd been told the Blue Ridge always were, a fact I didn't mention.

Dad, who had taken Thursday off from work to oversee the movers, went back to the plant Friday and as Mama told him good-bye she said in her cheery voice that we ought to be grateful to have had good weather while the furniture was being unloaded. My mother could usually find something to be pleased about. She and I tackled the packing crates again and by early afternoon the house was what she termed "reasonably straight," which meant the furniture was in position, sheets and towels put away, clothes sorted and in the right drawers and closets, and the glassware, china, pots and pans washed, dried, and on the shelves of the kitchen cabinets. Several unopened cardboard boxes remained stacked in the back hall but they could wait since they had nothing we needed at once.

"Let's stop for the time being, Christy," Mama said while she was warming canned soup for a late lunch. "We'll go into town and find a supermarket before the snow begins, and tonight we can have a real dinner at home. Bryan will like that."

"So will I." I smiled. My mother's cooking was far better than any food I'd tasted recently.

As we rode down our hill that gray January afternoon I didn't expect anything but a routine trip to the grocery store, and maybe it would have been exactly that, routine and nothing more, if we hadn't needed to fill the car's gasoline tank. Afterward, on the way to the house while I balanced egg cartons on my lap and stared at the first wet snowflakes hitting our clean windshield, I thought about the boy at the service station, recalling every single word he'd said, remembering how his eyebrows lifted to make small peaks when he smiled and how white his teeth were. His eyes were the same smoky shade of blue as the mountains on the previous morning in the sunshine.

Nobody could have been friendlier toward a stranger than the boy was to me. *I* was the one who muffed it. After he started the conversation, *I* wasn't able to keep it going and I hadn't even possessed sense enough to tell him my name. When he said he'd see me at school my silence must have given him the impression I was a snob or that I didn't care about knowing him better, and I didn't want him to believe either of those things. The longing to see him again was already turning into a tight little throb under my ribs though I realized I'd killed any chance of his wanting to be near me.

To my relief, Mama didn't mention the boy and I certainly didn't. I could discuss most matters with my mother, but not boys, since talking about boys meant owning up to the shame of only having had a very few dates in my entire life. Other girls my age didn't appear to be shy or awkward around boys, but I was and couldn't help it. The feeling gnawed at me and it hurt to think I must be practically the only sixteen-year-old girl in the world who wasn't a moron or hideously ugly who'd never had a real boyfriend.

Mama was aware of my lack of dates, of course, and I wasn't sure if it troubled her as she never mentioned it to me, but other people also knew and sometimes I had the feeling they must be snickering behind my back. The previous summer when we were in Indiana visiting relatives, Aunt Doris, my mother's oldest sister, asked if I was going steady or if I "ran around a lot with boys back home," as she phrased it.

She, Mama, and I were on her screened porch at twilight after a day which had been steamy and humid until an afternoon thunderstorm brought cooler temperatures, and I remembered staring at the shiny drops of rainwater clinging to shrubs in the yard. Aunt Doris' daughter, Francie, who was nineteen, had just ridden off in a white sports car with her date to go to a buffet supper party when my aunt put the terrible question about dating to me. I managed to shake my head, my throat suddenly so sandpapery it was impossible for me to make a sound.

"Oh well, Christy, maybe you're a late bloomer," Aunt Doris shrugged. "Some girls are. If you'll learn to open up more you *might* find a boy friend later on. You're truly different from your mother, though. Boys were tagging after Susan from the time she was in grade school. She — "

My mother cut in to talk about a dress she'd seen that morning in a store window, describing every button and seam and speaking so fast and so determinedly that Aunt Doris couldn't finish what she'd been about to say. I knew Mama was trying to spare me. For a moment I felt horrified that both of them knew so much about me and I inched my chair into the shadow of a huge planter of ferns so my face would be hidden.

That episode flashed through my mind on our first Friday afternoon in Greenview as Mama slowed the car to make the turn from the highway into our drive. Remembering Aunt Doris' biting statement about my possibly finding a boy friend later on if I learned to open up more made me cringe, and at the same moment I choked back a sigh. I had not learned. That was for sure. The way I'd acted with the boy at the service station was proof.

Dad came in an hour later, beaming at the sight of the table set for dinner and making a big thing out of peeping into the oven and lifting lids from the sauce pans on the stove to see what was cooking. "I think I'll bring in an armload of those logs stacked under the back steps and build a fire in the den," he said. "Once wood smoke is coming out of the chimney and the kitchen smells like food, that's home so far as I'm concerned."

My mother was across the kitchen taking

cucumber pickles from a jar with a long-handled fork and putting them into a square glass dish. She went to him, smiling and touching him gently on the cheek, and Dad slipped one arm around her waist and held out his other hand to me.

"Susan, Christy, you don't know how good it is to have you here," he added. "I've missed both of you more than you can guess these last few weeks. That motel made a poor substitute for my family and a home."

During dinner and afterward, while the three of us watched television, I pushed thoughts of myself away, especially the ones about my unintentional coldness to the boy at the service station, but all the aching memories returned once I was in bed in my room. On Thursday I'd been too tired to think about anything and I'd gone to sleep instantly, which wasn't the case Friday night when I was wide awake for a long time.

The silence surrounding me was eerie. If there was traffic on the highway, snow muffled the noise of cars and trucks. Flakes continued falling and the reflection of the white landscape made the cream-colored walls in my bedroom unusually bright in the darkness. I could make out my comb and brush on the chest of drawers opposite the bed and count the four notebooks from fall classes stacked on my desk across from the bay window.

After a while I got up and wrapped a blanket around my shoulders, sitting on the window seat which was built into the bay in my room. Outside, the sky was a luminous grayish-yellow with only one range of mountains visible. The trees in our yard looked as though they'd been upholstered in a cottony fluff and our hill was completely smooth and white without the barest indentation to mark the direction of the driveway. There was a loneliness in the wintery scene which matched my bleak feelings.

I don't know how long I sat there with my knees drawn to my chin, pulling the blanket closer and shivering a little as I peered through the bay window at the countryside. Chimney smoke and the smell of food cooking might make a house into a home for Dad, but I needed something more and wasn't sure what it would be.

Chapter

· 4 ·

Greenview High School was similar in appearance to a lot of other schools I'd attended, two-story, made of red bricks, and shaped like a capital E turned on its back. The athletic field was located at the rear, and on either side were parking areas paved with black asphalt, one for cars and the others for the buses to unload and load students. I could guess that inside the building the halls would be wide and classrooms would have rows of hard metal chairs, each seat with the arm expanded to make space for writing but never quite large enough for an open textbook as well as an open looseleaf notebook comfortably at the same time. Those guesses were correct.

One event made my first day at Greenview

High special. I saw *him*, the boy from the service station.

Despite my protests, Mama went with me to school that morning and insisted on going into the office to meet the principal. I said twice it wasn't necessary, my voice a little shrill the second time, and I wished secretly she would drop me off a block or two from school and let me walk the rest of the distance so other students wouldn't think I had to be shepherded like a third grader.

"There may be papers for me to sign and I can do them and be finished with them," she said, and from her tone I knew she'd already made up her mind.

She rummaged in her purse for the car keys as we trudged across the frozen ground in the backyard to the shed which served as a garage. Most of the Friday night snow had melted with just a few white patches left in shady spots and on the upper slopes of the mountains. The roads were clear and cars moved briskly on the highway below our hill.

"You drive, Christy," she said and gave the keys to me. I took them eagerly. At least I wouldn't be chauffeured right up to the school door, and if other students or teachers paid attention to my arrival at least they'd see that I had my driver's license.

Lots of girls and boys were on the school grounds, some heading for the entrance, others standing in groups, waiting for the warning bell before they went into the building. The air was cold and their breath made tiny curls of white mist near their mouths. They were laughing and gabbing the way old friends do and the sight made me aware all over again that I didn't know anybody. I gave those groups a quick glance and deliberately kept my eyes straight ahead.

"As soon as I finish here I'm going back home," Mama stated as I parked and passed the keys to her. "If you should miss your bus this afternoon, give me a call and I'll pick you up."

"Aren't you forgetting something?" I mumbled thinly. "Our phone hasn't been installed yet."

"The man from the telephone company is supposed to do it this morning. Christy" — she lowered her voice and put her hand on my wrist — "don't look so panicky. You're just as tense as you can be. It's not as though this was the first time you've ever been in a new school and it won't take long for you to feel at ease."

That sounded lovely when she said it, but I knew better. With all the effort I could muster I forced the corners of my mouth up into what I hoped was a smile.

Mama had nothing to sign and she left after introducing herself and me to Mr. Brady, the principal, a smallish man with gray hair carefully combed over a bald spot. He thanked us twice for Dad's notification of my enrollment as it gave him time to prepare my class schedule in advance and he gave me a boarding card with the number of my bus.

"I've assigned you to Mrs. Perkins' homeroom, room 218, and she's expecting you," he said. "It's at the far end of the building. I need to be in the office this time of day so I'll find a student to take you there. Wouldn't want you to get lost on your first morning with us." He smiled as he uttered the last sentence and went into the hall, leaving the office door open. From my chair I saw him stop a blond girl who must have just come in as she was bundled up in a brown coat and she carried an armload of books and notebooks which seemed to be slipping from her grasp, forcing her to tug at them. Her enormous round glasses gave her face an owlish expression.

"Christina Jamison," Mr. Brady said when he and the girl joined me, "this is Emily Halstead who'll show you to room 218."

The girl and I exchanged smiles and she shifted the books from her left arm to her right. "It's Christy," I corrected. "My name really is Christina but nobody uses that, thank goodness. I like Christy better." Mr. Brady took a ball point pen from his pocket of his shirt and scribbled "Christy" beside "Christina" on the outside of the folder holding my school records.

Emily began to chatter as soon as we were away from the office. "So you're new," she said. "Christy . . . mmmm. Cute name. How do you like the school?"

It was a dumb question and my, "Just fine," was routine. She should have known that if I didn't know the way to my homeroom I hadn't been around long enough to decide if I liked Greenview High or not, but I let that pass. "You're a senior?" she asked and when I said I was a junior, her lips pursed to form a little "O" and her round ·face with the round glasses and round mouth was a mass of circles. *"I'm* a senior," she added and for some reason I almost felt I should apologize for not being a year older than I was.

Emily pointed out things as we walked. "That's the library." She jerked her head toward a door. "The gym is under it in the basement, and the auditorium and cafeteria are at the back at the other end, next to where the buses are parked. Do you know which teachers you'll have?"

I held my schedule card out for her to see, watching her mouth become another "O." "Are you ever lucky because you have Mr. Hanson for math." She nodded so vigorously that the little blond curls on her forehead bobbed up and down. "He's a living doll, the only unmarried man under ninety-nine years old on the faculty. You can't win 'em all, though. You drew Miss Callahan for English. Ugh! Poor you. She'll work you to death. 'Nutty Nadine' is what everybody calls her and the best way to get along with her is to turn in *very* neat papers and *never* to be late for her classes. Never."

I made a mental note of the information. We passed throngs of students, some moving toward the stairs at the end of the long hall as we were doing, others coming from the opposite direction and facing us. Emily said hello to several people but didn't stop. I still had my pasted-on smile and it made my face feel like it was covered with plastic, although no matter how artificial it seemed, I vowed to myself to continue smiling all day.

When we had reached the stair landing, Emily's Spanish book slid out of the stack she was carrying and hit the floor with a flat *plop*! Both of us stooped to get it and as I straightened up and glanced ahead to the top of the flight, I saw *him,* the boy from the service station.

A strange tingling sensation enveloped me and I caught my breath. He was coming down the steps toward us, talking to a girl who walked beside him, gazing at her with an adoring expression on his face and no wonder, she was so beautiful. In that split second I noticed they were holding hands just as I took in her gold-flecked auburn hair and her gorgeous figure with curves in all the right places, yet I was really looking at him.

Everything happened so quickly that the entire incident was over almost before I knew it. He glanced away from the girl and I must have been staring at him because his eyes met mine and there was a flicker of recognition in the look he gave me. Maybe I continued walking. I don't know. I felt as if my feet were nailed to the stairs while the rest of me floated in outer space.

"Hi, there," he said. Somehow I got my mouth open to answer, "Hi," as he and the auburn-haired girl moved on past us, past the landing, going down the stairs. My coat was over my arm and I clutched it and my looseleaf notebook against my chest as if that would slow the way my heart was booming.

"You know Mike?" Emily asked in a surprised voice.

"Mike?" My voice was as odd as hers. It had been clear before, but now it sounded raspy.

"Mike Maxwell. That guy we just passed. He spoke to you, Christy."

She didn't mention that I'd also spoken to him and a terrible fear hit me. Maybe I hadn't been able to make a sound. Maybe I was only speaking inside myself because I wanted so much to be friendly to him, and he didn't know that and hadn't heard my "Hi," and would believe I hadn't returned his greeting.

Emily expected an answer and I made one. "My mother and I bought gas the other day and he was working at the service station," I said.

"Oh, I see. We get gas there, too. That's his uncle's business and Mike has worked there after school, and on Saturdays, and during the summers for ages." Her Spanish book was slipping once more and she pushed it back into the load. I wondered vaguely if she'd always had trouble carrying her books. "He and Jill really have a thing between them," she went on.

Jill had to be the auburn-haired girl with him, but I asked the question just the same.

"Jill Rogers." Emily's lower lip curled.

"That hair of hers is fantastic and don't think for a minute she doesn't know it. She practically has Mike under a spell."

"They're going steady?" My voice rasped again.

"Are they ever! They've been going steady since November when Vince Halloran quit school and left town. Vince had been dating Jill all fall."

I wanted to find out more about Mike Maxwell but didn't dare ask for fear Emily would discover how much I was drawn to him. Anyway, there was no time. She stopped walking, nodding her head toward the door of a classroom.

"Here we are. Room 218," she said. "Mrs. Perkins is sort of absent-minded so if she forgets to assign you a locker, remind her. I have to dash or I'll be late to my homeroom."

Chapter

· 5 ·

By the end of our first month in Greenview
my life was divided into two routines, and
some days I felt I was two separate people.
One was just another body occupying a chair
in class and another pair of legs walking the
halls of the high school, while the other
Christy Jamison was the girl who lived in a
house with nine bay windows, a house which
wasn't really home yet, although I received
a glowing welcome each afternoon at three-
thirty, when I stepped off the school bus.

My mother made the difference. She didn't
obviously watch for me — what I mean is,
she wasn't standing at the foot of our hill
or peeping out of the living room windows,
but she always called a cheery hello when I
came in. She'd been mostly by herself since
Dad and I left right after breakfast, which

41

made her full of conversation by the middle of the afternoon, ready to ask about my day and relate little happenings about hers. I knew she was as lonely as I was but neither of us referred to it.

We would sit at the kitchen table for a light snack, Mama mentioning unimportant incidents like seeing a man's sleeveless sweater in a shop window and that she thought she'd buy some yellow yarn to knit one like it for Dad; or commenting about the checker in the grocery store who was very, very pregnant and shouldn't be standing on her feet all day.

When Mama asked about school I said my classes were like those I'd been in in New York, and owned up to liking some teachers more than others, even to liking "Nutty Nadine" who wasn't as Emily Halstead pictured her to be. I had little to say about the students, though. The truth was that I didn't know much about them. The ones whose names I'd learned were polite and casually friendly without including me in their activities, and I wasn't dumb enough to expect to be part of a group until I'd lived in the town longer.

My mother never asked if I'd seen the boy from the service station so I supposed she'd forgotten him, and I didn't volunteer any information about Mike Maxwell. There wasn't much for me to have said except that I thought he was the nicest person I'd ever met and that he went steady with the prettiest girl at Greenview High. It was, I reflected more than once to myself, just as well that I didn't have to speak his name aloud. I couldn't even think it without having a fluttery feeling from my toes all the way to my hair.

Emily Halstead gave me a definite cold shoulder. During the first week I saw her in the cafeteria one noon and when I carried my tray of food to the vacant place beside her, she frowned, her face turning bright crimson and her mouth forming the little round "O" which I recalled from the morning she took me to room 218.

"Sit here if you like, Christy," she said with a shrug. "But this table is where seniors sit. I don't mean there are assigned places or anything like that, and it's a free world so you can go where you want, only there's a custom about this particular table and seniors using it."

I apologized, my face rosier than hers for a different reason, since her flush apparently came from annoyance that I'd bothered her and mine was from embarrassment. I tried to determine if I'd be less conspicuous moving to another spot or sticking it out for that one meal now that my tray was on the table. Going would be better, I decided. Besides, I wasn't hungry any longer.

"Thanks for letting me know, Emily," I murmured and my hands clutched the aluminum tray so tightly the skin was pulled taut across my knuckles until blue veins stood out on the backs of both hands. A girl named Betsy Collins, a junior like me who was in Mrs. Perkins' homeroom and also in my chemistry lab, motioned me to an empty seat at her table. I could have hugged her.

Greenview was so small that most of the students from town walked to school, while those with longer distances to go used the the buses, or drove cars, or rode with friends. Every afternoon when I was on the bus heading to my house I'd see Mike Maxwell getting into his car, a black sedan which looked to be eight or nine years old and was always in the same section of the parking lot. Jill invariably was with him and I could imagine he'd drop her off at her house a few blocks away and go on to his job at the service station. They held hands, so engrossed in each other they seemed to be on a planet of their own, despite the commotion nearby with students yelling, and car horns honking, and the yellow buses lumbering noisily toward the street.

I tried not to notice Mike and Jill and didn't succeed very well, just as I tried hard not to think about Mike Maxwell at all, reminding myself that I would never be anything to him except an acquaintance. His relationship with Jill was known and accepted as people said, "Mike and Jill this . . ." or, "Mike and Jill that . . ." It was never Mike *or* Jill and I told myself a million times that thinking about him even the tiniest bit was guaranteed to do nothing but keep my emotions churning.

Still, you can't completely ignore the person sitting behind you in a class and that was one reason I didn't have much luck with my determination to put Mike out of my mind. He and I had math together and Mr. Hanson, the teacher, seated students in alphabetical order, making everyone whose last name began with a letter coming after J move backwards one seat to make space for me. In that particular class there were no Ks or Ls and no other Js but me, so Jamison was immediately in front of Maxwell.

Just before math I had English, the two classes on the same hall, which meant I didn't have far to come and usually I was in Mr. Hanson's room when Mike arrived. He and I would say hello as he sat down behind me, putting his long legs on either side of my chair. In class most tall boys stretched out like that and some of the teachers objected to the aisles being cluttered — some girls objected, too — but I didn't mind.

It was fun being imprisoned by Mike's legs even though he didn't actually touch me or my chair. I'd glance down at the scuffed toes of his shoes and the hem of his jeans when I ought to have been concentrating on whatever Mr. Hanson was saying, wishing I could stare at Mike's face and memorize it the way I was able to study his feet. The few times we talked it was a quick conversation which he may have forgotten immediately or considered as nothing. I treasured every word.

I'd been at Greenview High about a week when he asked before math class began if I'd "settled in from moving," as he put it, and I assured him I had.

"I've never moved in my life," he came back. "Is moving good or bad?"

There was no opportunity for me to reply as the bell rang and Mr. Hanson started the lesson. All that day I had a warm, contented feeling and my smile wasn't the least bit forced because the question Mike asked about moving was proof he remembered my coming to the service station with Mama the previous Friday. Apparently he didn't hold my silence that first afternoon against me.

Thinking about it when I was in my room after dinner, I realized sadly that it wouldn't have made things any different between Mike and me if I hadn't acted stupid at the service station. I couldn't hold a candle to Jill Rogers. Getting up from the window seat in my bedroom, I stared at myself in the mirror over the chest of drawers. My figure was slim, almost boyish compared to Jill's, and I kept my hair clean but it didn't have the radiance hers had or the glimmering highlights.

Accept it, Christy Jamison, I said glumly to the girl who looked back at me from the mirror. *Jill has something that attracts boys whether it's sex appeal or beauty or charm or whatever. And you don't have it.*

On another morning Mike came to math muttering under his breath that he hadn't finished his homework the night before. He was early that day and other students were just starting to trickle in. I turned sideways in the chair, my pulse racing and the familiar

46

hot-cold tingle inching up my spine. That's how it always was when I was talking to him.

"You probably never have that situation with homework, Christy," he commented. "Girls always seem to do lessons on time."

I didn't want to appear smarter or more conscientious than he was. But I said the wrong thing. Afterward, I could have bitten my tongue off.

"Not always," I answered. "I thought it was a tough assignment, too. In fact, I didn't understand the final problems and don't think I'd have finished them, either, if I hadn't asked my dad for help. He's a whiz at math."

"Managing the electric motor plant means your old man's a brain, huh?" Mike's lips thinned out and his voice sounded caustic. "Must go with the territory, I guess. Mr. Harlow, the guy who used to be the manager there, was smart, too. If you didn't believe it he'd sure tell you how great he was. He was such a know-it-all, we hated to see him bring his car into the service station."

I didn't know what to say. My father was the most intelligent person I knew but I couldn't bear for Mike to think I was bragging any more than I wanted him to think Dad was a carbon copy of Mr. Harlow. All of a sudden I was tongue-tied, just as I'd been that first day when Mama and I bought gas, my palms damply warm and the rest of me icy. I don't know what I'd have done if Bud Warren, a friend of Mike's, hadn't come down the aisle.

Bud stepped over feet and made cracks about not being in the mood to run an obstacle course in math to reach his seat.

"It's good for your soul, Bud," Mike said, and grinned. "Hard on the rest of you but real good for your soul." As Bud passed by they nudged one another the way boys do, ignoring me, and I realized my conversation with Mike was over. I didn't know whether to feel sorry or relieved.

It wasn't so much that those little exchanges with Mike were important, but they were all I had in the way of contact with him which was why what happened toward the end of February was so unexpected.

Chapter

· 6 ·

If you want something to happen and it
doesn't, after a while the wanting becomes a
part of you like your eyebrows or your nose,
a thing you have, but take for granted.
That's how I felt about wanting fun on weekends, aching to have something lined up for
Friday or Saturday nights and knowing in
advance my fun probably would be a restaurant meal with Dad and Mama or seeing a
movie with them. It wasn't that I didn't enjoy going places with my parents; it was
simply that I hated missing out on what the
other teenagers were doing.

My lack of weekend plans was gnawing at
me that particular Friday afternoon toward
the end of February, because while I was
dressing after gym I'd overheard two girls
discussing the slumber party they were going

to that evening and how a bunch of boys were to crash "unexpectedly" at midnight. It sounded like fun and they laughed, rolling their eyes in anticipation. One of them, Mary Ruth Bennett, said she'd bought a pair of bright-red pajamas especially for the occasion.

"Maybe I'll upstage you and wear my sister's fishnet bikini," the other girl giggled. "That would make the fellows sit up and take notice."

"Take notice of an iceberg," Mary Ruth came back. "You'll freeze if you don't have anything on but a bikini in this weather, even if we are indoors."

That comment about freezing came back to me after the dismissal bell rang and I was hurrying toward the school bus. The afternoon seemed even colder than the frigid morning had been and a sharp gust of wind swirled my hair away from my face. I was reaching to the back of my neck to pull up the hood which was attached to my coat collar when someone called, "Christy! Hey, Christy Jamison — wait!"

Every muscle in my body tensed. It was Mike. He ran to catch up with me, taking leaping strides and weaving between the groups of students pouring out of school. The first thought to pop into my brain was how strange it seemed for Jill not to be with him. She was always at his side that time of day.

"Thought I'd missed you," Mike grinned as he reached me. He wasn't even breathing fast from the run. "I wondered if you'd like a ride home, Christy. My car's over there."

He gestured to the parking lot without taking his eyes from my face, and I was so stunned I couldn't think clearly. Mike Maxwell was offering *me* a ride when the school bus was only twenty feet from us, the bus I'd ridden all the other afternoons while he was driving Jill Rogers someplace. I couldn't take it in.

"How about it?" he said and his grin widened. It was easy to smile at him. I said, "Yes," and we started for his car.

He didn't take my books and I was glad, because holding on to those two textbooks and the looseleaf notebook gave me something to do with my hands. I was quivery with excitement. Nothing in the world could have thrilled me more than to have Mike seek me out, and at the same time I was puzzled. My mind seemed to be divided into tiny boxes with each box holding a question, only I couldn't ask him those questions.

Neither of us spoke until we reached the car. He opened the door on the passenger side and I sat down, smoothing my windblown hair and wishing desperately I had the courage to move over to the middle of the car seat to be really close to him, yet not able to make myself do it. I was leaning against my window, with my thigh pressing on the door handle and enough space in the center of the seat for a third person. Mike came around the front end of the car and I leaned past the steering wheel to pull the button by his window, unlocking the door for him, which gave me the chance to inch away from my window without being obvious about it. Plenty of space remained between us but not enough for anybody else unless that person was a dwarf.

"Thanks, Christy," he said. "Some people don't bother unlocking the door for a guy."

I couldn't tell if he liked my doing it or not, even though he'd thanked me. It was odd to be so dreadfully ill at ease with him and at the same moment so ecstatically happy.

The car motor sputtered and died. "Cold engine," he murmured and tried the ignition again. That time it caught and he whistled softly while he waited for the motor to warm up. I was almost dizzy with trying to think of something to say and like always when I was with a boy, my brain was blank.

"You haven't moved again, have you?" he asked. "I take it you're still living in the old Toscin house just outside of town."

"The one with all the crazy windows." I laughed too shrilly. "That's what you called the house and the description is perfect. I think about what you said every time I look through one of those bay windows."

Oh, glory, why did I have to say that? I thought frantically. I didn't want Mike to know how often I thought about him, or that I thought of him at all.

Mike put the car into reverse and backed out of the parking place, engrossed in looking over his shoulder to make sure he didn't hit anything, and I kept my eyes straight ahead even though the car turned. That was when I saw Jill Rogers. She was off the school grounds, moving briskly down the sidewalk with her shoulders unusually straight and the thin, wintry sunshine making her hair into a chestnut red crown. I watched her out of the corner of my eyes without seeming to stare, and as we drove past she deliberately turned her head, putting her back toward us. If Mike noticed her, he didn't let on.

"Christy, how do you like Greenview?" he asked.

"Fine. It's a nice place." It was my standard reply and I fell silent again. The subject seemed to be covered and just to be saying something, saying anything, I asked if his taking me home would make him late for his job.

"Nope. Uncle Eb doesn't expect me early and it's no sweat on weekdays as long as I'm there before four. As a rule we aren't real busy until later. I mean, not busy at the gas pumps. The service department is always in a rush."

The silence came back, that thick, embarrassing silence which was as loud between us as any noise would have been. He turned the car from the highway into our drive and it didn't matter any longer if I talked or not because the ride was practically over and I hadn't been a very interesting companion.

Blobs of ice lay around the north side of the trees in our yard and a few prickly brown balls clung to the branches of the sweet gum tree near the corner of the house. A scraggly gray bird pecking at the frozen earth soared into the air as the car approached.

"Dumb bird," Mike said. "Why didn't he fly south for the winter?"

"Maybe his wings don't work."

"They were flapping when he took off."

"Maybe he came here from someplace else and this is south to him," I said. "I came south and it's still cold to me."

"You didn't think you'd be getting Florida weather here, did you?"

"Not really. But I expected it to be a lot warmer than it is. I know Florida is a long way from Virginia but I didn't think Greenview would be practically as cold as where we lived in New York."

"I guess your house gets plenty of breeze on this hill, too." He braked by the porch steps without cutting off the motor. I had my hand on the door handle, my mouth open to thank him for the ride, when he said, "I wonder if you'd like to do something tonight, Christy."

"Do what?" I blurted out.

The instant I spoke I wanted to die. He was asking me for a date and I hadn't realized it. *Do what?* sounded as if I didn't want to be with him unless he promised excitement.

"Do whatever *you* want," he came back and winked at me.

My cheeks burned and I could imagine what he must be thinking. His mocking expression when he winked and the way he emphasized "you" implied he thought I was interested in a sexy evening, and even though I had no idea how sexy a time he anticipated, I had to let him know that wasn't what I meant.

"I-I just wanted to know — how to dress," I stammered. "If-If I should wrap up warmly. In case we're going to a ball game tonight."

Every remark I made sounded dumber than the previous one. Mike gave me an odd look. "This time of year it would be basketball and in the gym, Christy. Besides, our team's not playing this weekend. Didn't you know that? The schedule's posted on all the school bulletin boards." He slid the fingers of his right hand around the steering wheel until he'd made a complete circle. "I just thought we could go to Sonny's for a hamburger."

Sonny's was a soda shop type place in town where teenagers gathered and I'd been anxious to go there, but from what I'd heard mostly dating couples went or groups of kids. A boy could go by himself with no eyebrows raised and sometimes two or three girls might go together, but a girl who walked into Sonny's alone was advertising the fact that she wasn't cute enough to get a date.

I let my breath out slowly, trying to be sure that for once my answer was the right one. "Sonny's sounds like fun, Mike."

"Okay. I'll pick you up a little before eight.

I don't finish at the service station until seven and I'll have to go home and get cleaned up. Right now I'd better hit the road."

I watched him drive down the hill, realizing as he made the first bend in the lane that I hadn't thanked him for the ride. I'd do it that evening, I decided. It could be something to save for saying during one of those silences when our conversation lagged — if we had those silences at Sonny's.

For the first time in my life I had a feeling of self-confidence about being with a boy. Mike Maxwell had asked me for a date — he'd sought me out — he wanted to see me again — Mike Maxwell had asked me for a date — he'd sought me out — he wanted to see me again. The beautiful knowledge was like the refrain of a song and it spun round and round inside of me until I was positively giddy.

"Is that you, Christy?" Mama called as I let myself in.

Our house had the warm, tangy smell of cinnamon and nutmeg. My mother was cooking something good and on any other day I'd have gone straight to the kitchen for a taste, only that afternoon I needed a few moments to get myself together. I didn't want her to know how wildly excited I felt.

"I'm baking applesauce cookies," Mama came from the kitchen to the hall, where I was hanging my coat in the closet. "Was that a car, dear? I thought I heard one."

"A friend brought me home. I didn't ride the bus today."

"You should have invited her in. I wish you had."

Without looking at my mother, I knew she was smiling. It showed in her voice. She was pleased for me to have found a friend in Greenview and she was taking for granted I'd ridden home with a girl.

I made a huge job out of tucking my gloves into the pocket of my coat. "It was a boy, Mike Maxwell, and he couldn't stay because he had to go to work and he asked me for a date tonight to go to Sonny's." The words tumbled out, one syllable on top of the next so that I must have seemed breathless. That's how I felt. I hadn't thought to ask Mama if I could go with Mike. After all, I was sixteen. But I'd always been expected to ask permission if I wanted to leave the house at night, unless one or both of my parents were with me, and I knew if I didn't ask now and later my mother raised objections, the evening would be ruined.

"It's all right for me to go, isn't it?" I said and continued to press the gloves into my coat pocket.

"What's Sonny's, Christy?"

"Everybody goes there. Everybody from school. It's not a beer joint or a rough place. It's on Oak Street right behind the public library." My voice was squeaky because I wanted her to say yes, or nod, or do something which would indicate she didn't object so I wouldn't have to beg. If Mama said no, I'd die on the spot. "Mama, Mike's really super," I rattled on. "He sits behind me in math and he has a job after school and on Saturdays at the Greenview Service Station."

"Oh — that boy. He's Eben Maxwell's son?"

"Mr. Maxwell at the service station is Mike's uncle."

As I answered her it dawned on me I didn't know if Mike had a father or mother. I didn't know much of anything about him except that I liked him a lot, and it would be disastrous if my mother bombarded me with questions I couldn't answer.

For once, I was lucky. "Don't be later than eleven-thirty coming home tonight," she said and I went limp with relief. "I know it's Friday, but that's late enough unless it's a party or a special occasion."

It was a special occasion to me, my first date with Mike, and I didn't dare tell her how special it was. Not that she wouldn't have understood. My mother was extremely understanding, but if I continued to talk about Mike I'd give my feelings for him away and they weren't ready to be shared.

"Come on in the kitchen and get some cookies," she said. "I poured a glass of milk for you when I heard the front door open."

Saying I wanted to shampoo my hair, I ran upstairs without waiting for her to speak again. A glance in the mirror in my room told me how sparkly my eyes were and how pink my cheeks looked. My mouth felt uncommonly soft and moist. A kissable mouth? I hoped it was. It seemed almost ridiculous to think about kissing a boy I'd never actually been out with, but if Mike wanted to kiss me, I wouldn't object. He needn't know I'd never been kissed by a boy — really kissed, that is.

It wasn't until half an hour later, as I was standing in the shower with my hair a mass of wet suds and the warm soapy water was cascading over my shoulders and down my back, that I remembered I hadn't given Mama much of a reply when she said she had a glass of milk ready for me. Applesauce cookies were my favorite and she must have made that kind especially because I liked them. On any other afternoon I would have sat at the kitchen table, chatting with her while I munched cookies and drank milk, telling her things that happened at school, and listening to whatever she had to report about her activities. But that particular Friday, thinking about Mike and talking about him did such strange things to my throat I couldn't have swallowed a crumb.

I don't know what went wrong at Sonny's that night. It wasn't that I didn't have a good time because I did, and Mike couldn't have been nicer or more polite. Yet, something was definitely wrong, and afterward, trying to figure out what it was, I went over every word we uttered, every sentence Mike said to me, and what I said to him.

He was late reaching my house, almost nine o'clock, and my new self-confidence had faded in the fear that he might not show up at all. During dinner I'd managed to eat enough to keep Mama from asking if I felt all right and later I sat in the den with my parents and turned the pages of a magazine, unable to concentrate on the articles or stories, stealing glances at my watch for an endless time until the headlights of his car came into view through the bay window. Neither Mama nor Dad said anything about how late Mike was although I knew they were as much aware of it as I was. The doorbell finally rang and I jumped up, slowing my steps once I was in the hall alone. I drew a long, pulsating breath and made myself count to ten before opening the front door so I wouldn't appear too anxious to see him, and all the while my heart was thumping and banging against my ribs.

In my family it is unheard of not to introduce a friend and because it was important to me for my parents to approve of Mike, I was nervous when I led him into the den to meet them. Mama was working on the sleeveless yellow sweater and she stopped knitting, the long steel needles crisscrossed in the air with the yarn still wrapped around her fingers, and Dad tossed his newspaper to the floor and stood up. I needn't have worried about Mike making a good impression as he smiled his most charming smile at my mother and shook Dad's outstretched hand before turning to me in front of them to apologize for being late.

It seemed there was an automobile accident about six miles from town in the opposite direction from us and the state police radioed for a wrecker. "The call came when we were closing up and the other guys had already left the station for the night so I rode out with Uncle Eb," he explained. "I didn't have a chance to phone and tell you I'd be late, Christy."

I said it didn't matter, and strangely enough it didn't now that I knew he had a valid reason for being late. Dad inquired about the accident.

"Nobody was killed but two women were hurt and one car was totaled. None of the folks were from around here. One person can handle the wrecker in most cases but it's a lot quicker with two and Uncle Eb was half sick with a cold so I felt I ought to give him a hand."

A good sensation seeped through me. Mike wasn't an everyday sort of boy and my parents would have to be impressed with his manners and what he said about helping his uncle. The apprehension I'd built up during the wait for him began to vanish and some of my self-confidence returned. Not all of it, but some.

The night sky was black with a chilly-looking quarter moon directly overhead as we started for town, and Mike continued to talk about the accident until we turned into Oak Street. A red neon sign with "Sonny's" spelled out in rounded capital letters blinked on and off and so many cars were jammed around the one-story building we had to drive to the next block for a parking place.

"Ever been here before?" Mike asked and

I murmured that I hadn't. "I didn't think I'd seen you," he added. "It's fun. Not fancy, but fun."

Had he looked for me on other evenings? I'd have given anything to know but it's not the sort of question a girl can ask on a first date, especially a girl who isn't really at ease.

"I've heard Sonny's is wonderful and I'm anxious to see for myself," I said.

"They have a big lunch business with sandwiches and stuff, but at night it's mostly teenagers and they don't mind everybody staying until they close up. That is, if they behave. They'll throw you out if you make trouble."

"I'll try not to do anything to get myself thrown out," I said and giggled.

Mike exploded with laughter. "That would be the day, Christy. I can't imagine you ever cutting up. Cutting up in a bad way, I mean. You're not the type."

I longed to know what type he thought I was. Not a prude, I hoped. But not too free and easy with boys, either. I wasn't sure where the dividing line came between the two.

Inside Sonny's there was a narrow rectangular room with a soda fountain along one long wall and a row of booths opposite, while in the back, past a broad arch which was made to look like a garden trellis with green plastic vines trailing over it, was another room, that one square, with tables and chairs. The jukebox was playing a popular song hit and the laughter and chatter almost drowned out the loud music. Teenagers were everywhere, some sitting on counter stools by the soda fountain and others jamming the booths. I saw familiar faces from school and smiled at everybody while Mike nodded and gave a dozen hellos.

"We're too late for a booth tonight," Mike mumbled. "Guess we'll have to go to the back." He sounded as if he didn't care for the idea. I had no preference about where we sat; simply being there was enough for me.

As we walked under the arch with its plastic vines, someone from the corner of the back room yelled, "Hey, Mike! Over here!" It was Gordon Sager, a boy I scarcely knew, and he was with Betsy Collins, the girl who'd beckoned to me in the cafeteria the day Emily let me know I wasn't to sit with seniors. Gordon and Betsy were alone at a table for six and we joined them, Mike turning his straight wooden chair backwards and straddling it with his arms folded across the top.

Everybody laughed a lot and conversation was easy. We talked about TV shows, and movies, and school, with Gordon giving a priceless imitation of Nutty Nadine. I didn't feel new or strange and when Mike suggested a hamburger, adding that he was going to have two since he'd missed dinner because of the automobile wreck, I realized I was hungry. There was no table service and the boys went to the soda fountain for the food, leaving Betsy and me alone.

"Christy, how long have you been dating

Mike?" she asked as soon as Mike and Gordon were out of hearing.

I was thankful she lowered her voice so the people at the tables near us couldn't listen. The question caught me by surprise and I didn't know whether she was leading up to more questions or not. Betsy was a nice girl and at school she didn't have the reputation of being a gossip, but I was careful with my answer.

"I haven't *been* dating him at all," I said. "He invited me to come here tonight and here I am."

"I don't know what gives between him and Jill. They must have had a big blow-up to end all blow-ups if he's dating you — " She hushed abruptly, tiny red coin dots of color popping out all over her face. "I didn't mean that the way it sounded, Christy. It wasn't a slam at you. Honest. It's just really odd to see Mike with any girl except Jill, but I've always marveled at how he could put up with her disposition."

It was too much to have her discuss Mike and Jill — and me — right there in public. To change the subject, I complimented her on the brown and gold ski sweater she was wearing and we talked about clothes, but the happy glow from being at Sonny's was marred for me. It wasn't difficult to imagine what the kids near our table must be thinking or saying in undertones since Mike Maxwell wasn't with his regular girl.

The boys came back and I agreed with Mike that I'd never eaten a better hamburger. Three or four minutes later when I'd had several sips of Coke and was taking another bite of the sandwich, Gorden muttered, "Oh, ho, ho, ho. Guess who's heading over here."

The other three at our table were sitting so they could move their heads to look but my back was toward the entrance and I had to turn my body. Jill Rogers and Bud Warren had come through the trellis and were walking in our direction. The only empty seats in the back room were the two at our table.

That was when the evening fell apart.

The ground beef in my mouth wouldn't go down. I chewed and chewed, feeling almost nauseated as I nodded to the newcomers, wondering all the time if I'd have to keep the wad of food on my tongue forever. Jill, her hair shining as she moved her head, gave a huge smile and said, "Hi, gang," without asking if the vacant seats were being saved for anyone else. She took the chair to my right which meant I was between her and Mike who sat on my left at the end of the table. Gordon and Betsy were across from me, and Bud was at the far end, opposite Mike.

Mike gave a guttural hello to them and continued to eat, not paying attention to anything but his food. Jill took off her coat and carefully arranged it on the back of the chair so the hem wouldn't rest on the floor, which let me know she was at the table to stay. She was wearing a snug sweater the exact coppery red shade as her hair and I hated her because she was embarrassing Mike and ruining our fun. And because she was so beautiful.

The next twenty minutes were a nightmare. Mike spoke once or twice, his remarks for Bud or Gordon, not addressed to any of the three girls, and Jill laughed and chatted to no one in particular as if she'd never been happier or more carefree. I was stricken dumb. Finishing my hamburger was a physical impossibility and I laid what was left of it on the table while I played with the Coke, jiggling the ice around in the bottom of the paper cup until it melted and a watery brown liquid remained. Then I put my cold hands in my lap and held my purse in a death grip under the rim of the table. If I hadn't been on that wooden chair between Mike and Jill I felt sure they'd be talking to each other. Maybe they would be solving their problems and making peace.

Suddenly Mike jumped up. "Gosh, Christy, I forgot your curfew!" he said in a rough tone. "We'd best hit the road."

It was only twenty-five minutes past ten. I had an hour and five minutes before time to be home and besides, I'd never told him my mother set an eleven-thirty limit for me. I'd planned to mention that only if it was necessary.

Mike stood very tall, his fingers resting on the top of the chair back, waiting for me to do or say something. I got to my feet and managed to say, "Good night, everybody," without looking at any of them.

"Curfew? This early?" Jill gave a tinkling laugh. "You've got to be joking, Christy. Who has curfews anymore?"

Nobody answered her. She'd spoken loud enough to make heads at nearby tables turn and I hoped I didn't look as awkward as I felt. Mike walked off and I followed him across the square room, past the trellis and into the outer area. When we first arrived at Sonny's he'd made a point of holding the door so I could go in ahead of him and we'd walked side by side into the back, but it wasn't like that when we went out. He marched in front, taking such long steps I'd have had to dog trot to keep up which would have made me more conspicuous than ever so I walked at my usual pace. He flung the street door wide open, letting in a surge of cold air which made a group of girls in the front booth squeal, and that was when he glanced behind as though he'd just remembered I was with him. I still had several feet to cover to reach where he stood.

"Sorry, Christy." He bit the words out. "I thought you were here."

In the car I didn't know what to say or do. I wanted to tell him it was all right, that I didn't blame him for bringing me home early or for the evening being uncomfortable and turning out wrong. I even ached to say I understood how much he must want to be with Jill, but the words lumped in my throat and I couldn't get them out. Enough light came from the dashboard for me to see the way he clutched the steering wheel and I longed to reach out and cover one of those hands with mine. I didn't, of course. If he'd made even the slightest gesture toward me I'd have done it, but he sat as stiff as a fireplace poker, his chin jutting forward a little and his eyes on the road.

Mike drove fast and the trees and houses and streetlights whirled by until we were out of town on the dark stretch of road leading to our hill. There was almost no traffic. He hadn't turned on the car heater and I was so cold I was afraid my teeth would chatter, but I didn't mention it. He must have been warm. His coat was unbuttoned and his face had a shiny look as if he was perspiring.

As he slowed for our driveway he held his left wrist to the dashboard light to see his watch and I heard the small sigh he made, not more than a whispering sound. "Christy, I didn't realize it was this early," he said from between his rigid jaws.

"It's nearly eleven so it's not really early, but it's not late, either." I was trying to make everything all right, knowing nothing I did would help. "If you want to come in — " But Mike didn't wait for me to finish.

"I guess not tonight. Thanks, though," he muttered.

He braked by the porch, leaving the keys in the ignition with the motor running, a sure indication that he was anxious to go. Back to Sonny's and Jill? I wouldn't let myself think about it. It wasn't far for us to walk from the car to the house, not more than thirty or thirty-five feet, and that time

68

he matched his stride to mine, his hands in the hip pockets of his jeans with the thumbs sticking out and his coat still hanging open. Once he stepped on a dry twig which crackled as it split and the noise seemed unusually loud in the silence surrounding us. The wind had died and the moon was hidden behind wispy gray clouds, but we weren't in darkness as the porch light gleamed brightly and I wished it wasn't on because I didn't want to know about the misery showing on his face.

I found the house key in my purse and fitted it into the lock, the doorknob smooth and cold to my palm. "Mike, I had a good time," I said without looking directly at him. There was so much more I wanted to add. *Ask me again, Mike. Please. It'll be different next time. Better. I know it will.* Only I didn't utter a word and I pushed the front door open ever so slightly.

His "Sure, Christy. See you around" came as he ran to the car.

The warmth inside the hall didn't penetrate the chill I felt and I closed the door as quietly as possible, hoping for a few minutes to get myself together before Mama and Dad knew I'd come in. It didn't happen. My mother has fantastic hearing.

"That you, Christy?" she called. "If you and Mike are hungry there are lots of cookies in the kitchen. Orange juice, milk, and Cokes, too."

My tongue scraped over the roof of my mouth as dry as sandpaper. If I didn't go to them, Mama would follow me upstairs to make sure I was all right. Squeezing my eyes shut, I tried to will my heart to beat at a more even tempo.

"Christy . . . ?" Dad spoke that time.

"Coming. I'm hanging my coat up." I cleared my throat. "Mike had to go and I'm not hungry because we had hamburgers at Sonny's."

I stopped just inside the den doorway and watched my mother, who sat on the couch as she glanced away from her knitting, her eyes filled with expectation. She wanted to hear about my evening, and it wasn't mere curiosity on her part because she genuinely cared about what I did and that I enjoyed myself. An old John Wayne movie was showing on television, and Dad sat in the green-striped wing chair with his feet on the ottoman while he half-watched TV and worked the crossword puzzle in the newspaper. All of it seemed very normal and customary. I'd known in advance how they would be sitting and the way they'd look and what they would be doing, and for some strange reason the turmoil inside of me increased at the sight of their calmness.

"Did you have a good time, dear?" Mama asked. "Mike seems like a very nice boy."

He is. Oh, he is, I ached to tell her. Instead, I fibbed. I couldn't explain to them about the evening and how awful it had turned out, and lying was the easiest answer.

"Everything was fun," I said. "Mike had

to leave because he gets up real early Saturdays and he works all day at the service station. I'm going to my room because I have a book report due Monday and forgot all about it until now and I haven't even opened the book. Maybe I can get a few chapters done tonight rather than leaving the whole thing for the weekend."

Sometimes I can read my mother's mind, and the way she smiled let me know instinctively that she thought I had plans to go out with Mike Saturday or Sunday and was getting my lesson assignments out of the way. I needed to set her straight and couldn't make myself say anything else except good night.

For a little while after I was upstairs in my bedroom I sat on the window seat without undressing or turning on a lamp. The clouds had moved away from the face of the moon, and beyond the road and pastureland, the mountains were hidden against the black sky. I was furious with myself for telling fibs. It wasn't necessary to give Mama and Dad a detailed account of the evening, but I didn't have to invent a book report or make excuses because Mike left early. It had been years since I'd lied to my parents, not since I was a very small girl, and to realize I'd done it that night was humiliating.

But I couldn't even think Mike's name without trembling inside, much less say it aloud, and if my mother asked when I was seeing him again I was afraid I'd cry. He wouldn't phone me about our getting together Saturday or Sunday. I was positive he wouldn't.

And he didn't.

At school Monday, Mike was late coming to math. His "Hi, Christy" was drowned by the bell, and he spoke without looking at me, although he must have felt my eyes on him as he walked down the aisle or he wouldn't have bothered to say anything. I couldn't concentrate on math that morning. If Mike leaned forward just a little his breath fluttered on the back of my neck. He didn't sprawl in his seat or spread his legs out on either side of my chair, and at the end of class he popped up like a jack-in-the-box, the first person out of the room.

During lunch I ate with Betsy who chatted a mile a minute about everything under the sun — except Mike. *Please tell me,* I begged her silently. *Did he return to Sonny's after he took me home? Did you see him over the weekend and what was he doing and was he with a girl? With Jill?* Any little tidbit of information was better than knowing nothing and when I finally mustered the courage to ask, some girls Betsy knew brought their trays to our table and sat opposite us and then Gordon Sager sauntered over, so I kept quiet.

I couldn't believe Mike would be low enough to use me, asking me out simply to make Jill jealous if they'd had a fight and broken up. If he hadn't liked me on the ride from school Friday afternoon, would he have made the date for that night? Would he?

Thinking about it bolstered my self-esteem a little, and the nagging thought persisted that if I could talk to him for just a few minutes I'd be able to straighten out whatever was awkward between us, although I had no idea what to say to him. At least he would know I wasn't angry.

I didn't see him at school any more that day and even if I had, I might not have had the nerve to walk up to him and start a conversation. But there was almost an opportunity to do it later in the afternoon. Almost. It was one of those moments when wanting a thing to happen, wanting it desperately, doesn't make it come true.

My mother was cooking a pot roast for dinner when I came in from school, frowning because she didn't have any onions to flavor the gravy.

"Christy, would you go to the grocery store for me?" she asked. "Get the onions and you'd better buy some milk at the same time. Take my billfold. It's with the car keys in my purse."

For the first time that Monday a little of my inner turmoil lessened, and as I got into the car I felt warm all over at the realization that it was now possible to see Mike without being obvious about it. I'd go to the Greenview Service Station and buy gasoline, even paying with my own money, not Mama's. It would be worth the bite out of my allowance to talk to him.

Then I looked at the gas gauge and a huge weight seemed to slam down on my head. The red arrow pointed to "Full." For the only time in my life I wished a tire would go flat or the fan belt would break or the antifreeze would drain out, anything to make me need to call the service station for help.

Instead, I bought half a gallon of milk and four onions at the supermarket and drove back to the house.

The answer to one of my questions about Mike came accidentally, twenty-four hours later, on Tuesday when he left school with Jill, holding her hand and gazing down at her, laughing at whatever she was telling him. I was on the bus and I watched them through the window, unable to turn my eyes in another direction.

Every time she moved her head her hair swung from side to side like a colorful silk scarf. The two of them got into his car, Jill sitting in the middle of the front seat, close enough for her shoulder to touch his. She was still laughing and making him laugh as the school bus moved forward out of the parking lot and into the street.

I began to ache. My head hurt, my back, even my hands and feet throbbed, and all of it came from the haunting knowledge that nothing would develop between Mike and me. I had to stop thinking about him, I told myself over and over. I must not even think about him again, and all the while I knew it was an order to be disobeyed. You can't flip your heart off and on like a water faucet.

Until that moment I'd been sure Jill was to blame for the dismal events Friday night. Now, I knew better. After seeing Mike with her I was aware that part of the trouble — maybe most of it — had to be my fault. Other girls knew how to interest boys, how to make them laugh, to put them at ease. I lacked that ability. I'd had my chance with Mike Maxwell and failed because I hadn't proved to be the kind of date he wanted.

talking about her garden since the day we
arrived in Virginia, became positively ecstatic on the subject in March, when the

Chapter

· 7 ·

My mother, who had been planning and talking about her garden since the day we arrived in Virginia, became positively ecstatic on the subject in March, when the weather turned unseasonably mild and early jonquils bloomed in the yard. The vivid yellow flowers were scattered over our hillside, small and on short stems with two or three in a cluster.

The garden plans came up again one Wednesday night in late March while we were eating dinner. Dad and Mama had been talking about making a flagstone walk from the back door to the rear of the yard where Mama's garden was to be, Dad maintaining that it would be difficult since the walk must go downhill and Mama insisting it was worth a try. I more or less listened while I was thinking about the flowers and the changing seasons and how pleasant our kitchen was. Some nights we ate in the dining room, a barn of a place, while the kitchen was cozy and comfortable, and if I set the table I usually chose the kitchen.

My eyes moved from one corner of the kitchen to the next, enjoying what I saw. A row of blue and white Dutch tiles hung on the wall near the stove and an African violet plant in a cream-colored ceramic pot sat on the windowsill over the sink, the purple flowers growing in a little circle banked by fuzzy green leaves. With the days becoming longer, the last of a coral sunset was visible through the bay window where our table had been put to give us a view of the mountains during mealtimes.

Every day for a week there had been fresh signs of spring. The grass was changing from rusty brown to a definite greenish color and the dogwood buds had begun to swell. I'd examined the oak tree outside my bedroom window, not finding any hint of leaves yet, although the branches seemed different from their January and February starkness — softer looking — and the bark not so sooty black. It didn't matter that the nights were still cold since the recent daytime temperatures were lovely, and after such a bitterly frigid winter it was nice to go outside in the afternoon without having to bundle up to my ears.

We finished eating that Wednesday night and I carried the dishes to the sink, everything except my parents' coffee cups. Mama remarked that she wanted to have a flower bed near the kitchen window in addition to the large garden.

"Something colorful that'll survive the summer heat and won't need much weeding, but will look pretty from inside the house as well as to anyone driving up from the highway," she went on. "Bryan," she addressed Dad, "I'd like to get my main garden area plowed right away. The ground is packed too hard for me to turn the soil over by hand, so will you find somebody with a tractor to do it?"

"You shouldn't plant seeds this early," he said. "I know you're eager to start digging but we'll have more cold weather."

"The earth ought to be aerated. That should be done in the early spring before planting."

He grinned at her and took another swallow of coffee. "Do you have a blueprint for the plowman to follow, Susan?"

She made a face at him and all three of us laughed. My mother's "garden blueprints," as Dad called them, were in an old spiral notebook I no longer needed at school. She tore out the used pages and on the remaining sheets drew outlines of where she would put certain vegetables and which flowers she wanted in a particular spot, changing her mind and making new sketches every time a new seed catalogue arrived in the mail.

"Perhaps you could get one of the men from the motor plant to do the plowing," she suggested. "During his off duty hours, of course."

"I'd hate to ask any of them. If the boss — in this case, me — makes a request, it's a command and hard to refuse. I don't want to put any of the company people on a hot spot, especially when I'm just beginning to live down some of the problems Ira Harlow created." Dad finished his coffee and put his hand lightly on my mother's shoulder as he walked by her chair. "I'll inquire around, Susan. Eben Maxwell knows everyone in the area and he can probably give me the name of somebody."

The word *Maxwell* made my face instantly stiff and I was thankful to be scraping plates at the sink with my back toward Mama and Dad. Merely hearing the name was unnerving. In the three and a half weeks since our one date, Mike and I had returned to the same casual relationship we had before he took me to Sonny's. We exchanged hellos if we passed in the hall at school and occasionally we talked a little when we were waiting for math class to start, neither of us mentioning our evening together. I wondered if he'd forgotten it. There was no reason for me to go to the service station, as each time I drove Mama's car the tank was full or almost full and besides, Mike was dating Jill. I'd seen them together in the school cafeteria and coming out of the building.

Dad announced at dinner the next evening that Eben Maxwell had arranged for a man named Charlie Jordan to plow up Mama's garden and that he would be out very early Saturday morning, unless it was raining. My mother looked as pleased as if she'd been handed a basket of money, but I couldn't take time to dwell on it as I had two tests coming up and a paper due for English. Knowing how busy I was, Mama volunteered to wash the dinner dishes for me.

Chapter

· 8 ·

Saturday, like the days immediately before, was sunny and springlike without a speck of cloud in the blue sky and my mother should have been overjoyed, but when I came downstairs that morning she was storming around the kitchen in a terrible mood. I'd slept late as I did most weekends and it was past ten o'clock. Mr. Jordan hadn't put in an appearance.

"I thought he was to be here *early*. This makes me furious." She had an edge to her voice. "Your father got up at six and staked off the section to be plowed so Mr. Jordan won't have to do any measuring, just plow, and it's less than two hours work with a tractor and we'll pay him well. The man said he'd be here." It wasn't often that my mother showed so much irritation, but one thing she couldn't abide was a broken promise without a good reason.

"Did you try phoning Mr. Jordan?" I asked. "Maybe he forgot it or maybe he doesn't know where we live." I put two slices of bread in the toaster, poured myself a glass of orange juice, and took the jar of strawberry jam from the refrigerator.

"Everybody in this section knows the Toscin house because of the windows and he could find us if he made the effort." She gave a small sigh. "I don't know how to get in touch with him."

"Doesn't Dad have an address for him? Or a phone number?"

"I doubt it. Bryan had to go to the plant this morning even though he's hoping to play golf at one o'clock. I hate to upset his day. If Mr. Jordan doesn't come by noon, I think I'll give Eben Maxwell a call. He'll be able to tell me how to locate the man."

I spread a spoonful of jam on my toast, relishing the taste of warm butter with the syrupy red fruit. Mama continued to murmur about her garden and Mr. Jordan's lackadaisical approach to doing what he said he would do.

"The radio has forecast rain for tonight and said a cold wave is heading in our direction," she went on. "If Mr. Jordan doesn't show up and it turns cold enough for the ground to freeze, heaven knows how long it will be before any plowing can be done."

The window over the sink was open a few inches and the air which came in was as balmy as May. I scanned the sky, seeing nothing but brilliant blue, with the mountains so clearly outlined I could almost pick out individual trees. It was hard to believe we might have rain in a few hours or that the temperature was supposed to drop sharply, not on such a golden morning, but I didn't say any of those things to Mama. I was hoping she'd talk her irritations out of her system and return to being her normal, cheerful self in a hurry.

I finished breakfast and since she didn't have any immediate chores I went outside, strolling across the backyard to the outcropping of rocks between the house and the garden-to-be. It was a lazy morning — what was left of it. Having had a late breakfast, I didn't want a real lunch, so Mama and I ate hard-boiled eggs and applesauce and drank a pot of tea. Her disposition was better since her noon telephone conversation with Mr. Maxwell. He was genuinely upset that Charlie Jordan hadn't come or sent a message, she reported, and he assured her he would have her garden done before bedtime if he had to plow it himself in the moonlight.

By four o'clock her glum irritation had returned. She gave an exasperated moan and announced that she'd wasted most of the day waiting so she might as well go on and wash her hair and not have the entire Saturday be a loss, since Eben Maxwell was apparently no more reliable than "that Charlie Jordan." I wanted to defend Mr. Maxwell just because he was Mike's uncle, reminding Mama that

Saturday is one of the busiest times for men who earn their living repairing cars, but I didn't. It seemed wiser to let the matter drop.

In a few minutes I heard the shower running and had a whiff of the herb shampoo she used. I sat down at the desk in my room and was opening my math book to start on Monday's assignment when I heard what sounded like a car engine and looked out to see a red pickup truck coming up our hill, with "Greenview Service Station" printed on the side in tall white letters. It moved slowly because of a small tractor attached by a chain to a trailer hitch on the rear bumper.

"Mama, the man's here," I sang out. The pickup had gone past my range of vision, although I could see the end of the tractor.

She turned the water off and poked her wet head around the shower curtain. "I'm dripping and haven't finished my hair, Christy. Show him the garden so he can get started."

I went through the kitchen and out of the back door to find Mike sliding from under the steering wheel of the red truck. The sight of him startled me so much I could only stand on the next to bottom step where I'd stopped, a foolish little smile on my face.

"Hi, there," he said and grinned just as he had done that first afternoon at the service station. "I think I'm supposed to play farmer today."

"My mother wants her garden plowed. It's where you see the red flags." With one hand

I gestured to the stakes that held the red markers, my eyes on Mike and my voice unaccustomedly breathless. "I though a man named Jordan was coming to do the plowing."

Mike leaned against the front fender of the truck. "Well, it's like this," he said. "Charlie Jordan picked last night to get drunk and he's not in navigating condition today. Charlie's okay when he's sober. You'll never see a nicer guy or a harder worker. He used to drink a lot but he quit three or four years ago and hasn't touched a drop since — not that anybody knew about — until last night. Uncle Eb is darned mad about it, too. He promised your folks somebody would show up today to do your garden, so I'm the one."

I must have appeared silly staring at him in silence, my hands clasped behind my back. There was so much I wanted to say and I couldn't think of any of it, the crazy thought spinning in my head being the wish that I had on makeup and perfume and was wearing something more glamorous than jeans and an old plaid blouse which had seen better days. All the time I knew it didn't matter what I was wearing because Mike hadn't come to see me, just to work. He was in jeans and a gray sweatshirt with G.H.S. for Greenview High School in black letters across the front.

"Any special instructions?" he asked.

I murmured no. He seemed to be waiting for me to say something else and when I didn't, he climbed into the truck and drove off toward the garden, the tractor swinging along behind. Stopping beyond the big rocks, he got out and walked to the back of the truck to release the chain, then sat on the tractor seat and started the engine.

I went in the house because I didn't know what else to do. *I won't watch him, I won't,* I told myself. I did, though, first from the living room window and then from the bay window in the kitchen, taking care to stand far to one side so he wouldn't spot me if he glanced at the house. He sat very straight on the tractor seat, his shoulders erect while thick dust swirled up from the ground behind him, and it must have been a bumpy ride because sometimes he bounced. Once I saw him rub his eye as though he had a speck in it, and another time he slid the knuckles of his left hand across his mouth.

The raucous, grating noise of the tractor engine was loud all the way to the kitchen, which I guess was why I didn't hear Mama or realize she was a few feet behind me until she spoke. In a tan jumper and a white blouse she looked pretty and fresh.

"I see Mr. Jordan didn't waste much time when he finally got here," she said. "Did he tell you why he was so late?"

I knew my voice would squeak and it did. Talking about Mike always caused that to happen. "It's not Mr. Jordan, Mama. He got drunk last night and apparently he has a hangover today."

"Then who — ?"

"Mike. His uncle sent him." I squeaked once more, a Minnie Mouse voice.

My mother had to be aware of how odd I sounded but she didn't mention it, and she peered through the window at Mike who was finishing a row. He made a wide, sweeping turn with the tractor, the dust so thick it was obvious why she failed to recognize him from a distance.

"I knew it was dry but didn't realize quite how dry," she commented.

Using homework assignments as an excuse, I went upstairs to my room. It wasn't that I didn't want to see Mike because I did, but it was impossible to forget he'd dropped me flat after one date . . . only one. No girl could go through the hurt of that without cringing at the memory. It was painful at the time and it was still painful four weeks later.

Mama had never asked about what happened between Mike and me at Sonny's although I imagined she wanted to know. She hadn't forgotten that one date any more than I had, as she seldom forgot anything, and maybe she thought it was unusual for me not to confide in her since I talked to her about most other things, but some feelings are too deep and personal to discuss at all.

There was another reason why I couldn't mention my lack of dates to her. She'd been very popular with boys when she was in high school. Aunt Doris made that clear, and I doubted if my mother would understand how it was with me. She didn't know the embarrassment of staying home every Saturday night, or going to the movies with her parents, or the bittersweet agony of wanting a boy to like her and finding herself turning to stone if she had the chance to be with him. I couldn't talk to her about Mike any more than I could stand at the kitchen window with her and pretend he was merely a boy I knew casually at school, not when my pulse was racing at the straightness of his back and the way his dark hair was pushed off his forehead.

An hour inched by. I moved restlessly from the desk chair to the window seat in my room and back to the chair, ignoring school books and homework. The tractor continued to make its chugging, grumbling racket.

"Christy," Mama called from downstairs, "Mike ought to be ready for a breather. How about taking him a Coke?"

It wasn't actually a question although it sounded like one, but it was her way of issuing an order. My stomach muscles wrenched sharply. For a moment I felt as if I'd been hit under the ribs and I had to make myself get up from the chair. My mother would call me again if I didn't come and it seemed less embarrassing to follow her instructions and do it quickly than to make an issue. I would hand Mike a Coke and return to the house immediately, I decided.

When I reached the kitchen she was cracking English walnuts with an old brass nutcracker which had belonged to her father.

Without saying anything, I took a can of Coke from the refrigerator and started out of the back door.

"For heaven's sake, Christy!" Her voice was tinged with annoyance. "Take along one for yourself so you can talk to Mike while he's drinking his!"

In the warm room I was suddenly icy cold. *He doesn't want me . . . he dropped me after one date . . .* The words gnawed at my heart.

"I-I — He might not — not like that," I said in a jerky way. "I-I guess he's anxious to — finish and leave."

The nut in her hand went *crack!* when she squeezed the cracker too hard and the shell scattered on the floor. Glad to be able to duck down, I gathered up the broken pieces, and while I was doing it my mother was taking a second Coke from the refrigerator. She handed it to me and I couldn't avoid her eyes any longer.

She understood how I felt. I knew it. I saw the tenderness in her face and the soft sympathy for another person's hurt.

"Christy, when I was sixteen I was just as shy with boys as I could be," she said gently. "I didn't know then that boys are shy, too, even the ones who seem very sure of themselves. If Mike doesn't want the Coke or if he's in such a rush he can't chat a few minutes, you'll know it. But give him a chance. At least have a drink for yourself just in case."

With my cheeks flaming as red as the bright-red Coke cans, I stepped outside. Mike saw me coming and cut off the tractor engine in the middle of the row, leaping to the ground, and by the time I was near the big rocks he was walking toward me.

"You must know how dry I am," he said. "I've got grit in my nose and mouth. My ears, too, I guess. I sure hope one of those drinks is for me."

"For nobody else." I held out the can to him and he took it, his fingers grazing mine ever so slightly. He pulled the tab and had a huge gulp. "You've made my mother's day by plowing her garden," I told him just to be saying something. "It's a big deal for her."

"She'll wish she'd laid out a smaller plot when she begins hoeing and fertilizing. Are you going to help her?"

"A little, I guess. She wants to plant vegetables as well as flowers."

"Now I'll know where to come next summer when I want a fresh cucumber or a ripe tomato," he said.

It wasn't a funny remark but he laughed. I felt lighthearted, so much at ease I didn't worry about anything. "Does your family raise a garden, Mike?" I asked.

"Not really. Uncle Eb usually has a few rows of sweet corn in the vacant lot next to the station and he ends up giving most of it to Mom and Dad. That means to me, of course."

"Oh — you don't live with your uncle?"

"Whatever gave you the idea I did? Heck, no. I live with my parents the same as you do with yours." He took another long swallow of Coke. "I take it you're an only child."

"Sure am," I laughed. "You mean it shows that I'm spoiled? Aren't all 'only children' supposed to be spoiled, rotten brats?"

I expected a teasing reply from him and to my amazement, he spoke seriously. "You're not rotten or a brat, Christy. I'd say you're just the opposite. Come to think of it, I might as well be an only child. I have two brothers but I guess I was an afterthought because my brothers are so much older than I am that they left home when I was in grammar school." He crushed the empty can between the heels of his hands. "Well, I'd better get back to work. I think I've done all the damage I can to this Coke."

He tossed the crumpled can into the back of the pickup and started for the garden. Then he turned to look at me. "Ever ridden a tractor, Christy?"

I shook my head.

"Want to give it a go?"

My yes came promptly and I scampered over the furrows, my sneakers leaving footprints on the powdery earth. Mike got on the tractor first and I realized there was only one seat, a bucket-type metal scoop.

"I don't think there's enough room for two," I said and my disappointment showed.

"Want to bet? Sure, there's room. Right here." He spread his legs and pointed to the space between them, giving me a hand up. I sat down, my legs against his legs and my back resting on his chest. He had to look over my shoulder and around my head to see forward, which made his cheek almost touch mine and that side of my face tingled.

"Ready?" he asked and turned on the engine. With both of his hands on the steering wheel, his arms were on either side of my body and I could hear his heart going thud-thud-thud against my spine.

We jolted off and I reached out automatically to hold the steering wheel so I'd keep my balance. Mike stopped the tractor at once.

"You'll flip us over if you do that," he warned. "I'll drive and you ride. Okay? Nobody's hands on the wheel except mine."

"But I need to hold something so I won't fall off!"

"Hold my knees."

I did, trying not to let my fingers claw him but the earth was packed hard and it was a rough ride. A fun ride, too, in spite of the dust rising into my face and the bounces. I squealed once on a particularly uneven spot and Mike chuckled. I felt his laughter as much as I heard it, the sound coming from deep in his chest.

"Hang on, Christy!" he yelled when he reached the end of the row and swung the tractor in a U-turn. He had to move his arms against my sides to keep me on the seat and it was a delicious sensation. I felt completely safe. Nothing could make me fall with Mike holding me.

We were into the final row before I noticed the sun was out of sight behind the mountains and the sky had turned a mottled gray without any blue or sunset colors. Until that moment I hadn't realized the fair weather was changing to cloudiness or that the air was definitely cooler.

Yet, with darkness coming, I could imagine he was eager to finish and my being on the tractor must be slowing his work. "Am I in the way?" I asked. "I'll get off if you like."

"I don't like. You stay where you are — unless you're uncomfortable."

I doubt that I was actually comfortable but I didn't mind, and the nearness of his arms with the solid feel of his chest against my back more than made up for my unsteady perch. The last row went too quickly. When it was finished he pulled the tractor to the rear of the truck and secured it with the chain to the trailer hitch.

"Want a lift to the house, Christy?" he asked.

"I'd love it. Are you planning to make me ride the tractor by myself?"

It was a silly question and he knew I was kidding. He flashed a grin and said, "I don't think so. Not today. I was counting on your being in the pickup with me."

Everything was so easy and natural between us I was sure he intended suggesting that we do something that evening. We could stay in the living room at my house or see a movie or go to Sonny's. It didn't matter to me what we did or where we went so long as we were together.

I stole a look at him as he drove the short

distance to the house. Dust clung to his lashes and eyebrows and I fought the urge to reach over and rub off the gray smear of dirt on his jaw. I waited for him to mention a date, and when he didn't, a terrible uneasiness swept through me. *Ask me now,* I begged silently. *Don't keep me in suspense, Mike. We had fun on the tractor and we'll have fun tonight.* I wanted him to know I longed to be with him and how much I'd enjoyed the afternoon, only the part of my mind which did thinking and the part which formed words were strangely disconnected and I couldn't say anything.

He stopped the truck by the back steps and Mama came out of the house, standing with the open door behind her so that she was silhouetted against the light from the kitchen. Her hair was fluffy around her face.

"Thanks, Mike," she said. "You did a beautiful job. Tell me what I owe and I'll write you a check."

"That's between you and Uncle Eb, Mrs. Jamison. You pay him."

She told him she'd take care of it first thing Monday and went in the house once more, leaving Mike and me alone in the gray twilight. I knew I couldn't continue to sit there beside him and wait. *Ask me, Mike. Go on and do it now . . . please.* I thanked him for the tractor ride and there was a little hope left in me until he said, "I guess I'll shove off since it's getting dark."

He leaned across me to open the door on

my side and I got out, standing on the ground trying to smile, although I wasn't sure my lips were curving. My face felt rigid. "It was great fun," I murmured. Anything to hold him a tiny bit longer.

"Yeah. I thought so, too, Christy."

But not enough for you to want to be with me again, was it? He was in a hurry to leave so he could see Jill. He hadn't said it but I could guess and all the happiness I'd experienced from the moment I handed him the Coke disappeared as if it never existed.

Mike waved and drove off, braking at the end of the yard before he started down the hill to let Dad, who was coming in, to pass by. Dad stopped his car beside the truck to speak to Mike, the headlights of the two vehicles sending crisscrossing beams in both directions. I was too far from them to overhear what they said to one another and I was chilled all over, but I didn't want to leave the yard until Mike was out of sight, in case he changed his mind and returned. He wouldn't. I was sure he wouldn't . . . but sometimes miracles happened.

Too, I needed a little more time to get my features into a normal expression so my mother wouldn't see how disappointed I felt.

Mama was stirring something in a saucepan on the stove and as I came in she glanced at me and laughed. "Go look at yourself in the mirror, Christy," she said. "You haven't been this dirty since you outgrew mud pies. You're covered with dust from your head to your feet. And leave those sneakers here in the kitchen until you clean them so you won't track dirt all over the house."

I untied my shoes and slipped them off, asking if there was time for me to have a bath before we ate and she said yes. She laid the wooden stirring spoon on a paper towel and put the lid on the sauce pan, and I knew she was waiting for me to mention Mike. Ten minutes earlier I could have done it and thanked her for insisting on my carrying two Cokes to the backyard instead of just one, but that was when I was glowing from the nearness of him and when I expected him to want to see me again very soon. Now, I didn't say anything and the unasked questions were in her eyes.

Chapter

· 9 ·

I wasn't conscious of having dreamed about Mike, although I'd have liked to, but I was thinking about him when I woke up Sunday morning, the hazy thoughts so pleasant I wanted to hold them close as long as possible. Lying in bed, my eyes remained shut after my mind was rid of the sleep mist and I relived the time on the tractor with my back resting against his chest and his breath on my cheek. I knew exactly how his hands looked holding the steering wheel, and that the right sleeve of his sweat shirt had a tear about an inch long at the wrist, and I remembered the clean glossy shine of his hair until dust covered it, and how intently he looked at me when he was drinking his Coke.

If a person likes or dislikes you a lot you know it instinctively and the previous afternoon I could sense Mike's liking for me. Nobody forced him to ask if I wanted a ride on the tractor. It was his idea, a fact I'd reminded myself of a hundred times. Yet, the chilling memory always returned that he didn't suggest our getting together again. That was the part which hurt. I'd been so sure when we got into the truck after the garden was plowed, so very, very sure of him, and it was a raw jab of pain to hear him say, "I guess I'll shove off since it's getting dark," as though he couldn't get away from me quickly enough.

Maybe *I* should have suggested a date. At least I could have invited him into the house. No, I couldn't, I decided. It was hard enough watching him drive off but it would have been worse if I'd given him an invitation and he'd turned it down. My taking the initiative would have meant I'd forgotten his dropping me after the Friday at Sonny's, and I couldn't forget. The recollection came surging forth and with it, the familiar aftermath of desolation.

With tremendous effort I shoved those thoughts aside and opened my eyes. The door from my bedroom leading into the hall was closed and my room was uncommonly bright without sunshine. The silence was eerie, an overwhelming hush so vast I heard nothing but my own breathing. No tree branches rattled and there was no hum of traffic from the highway. I sat bolt upright in bed and knew what must be happening even before I looked out of the window, because only one thing brought that strange silence along with the brilliant reflection of light which spilled into every corner of the room. Snow!

I gave a small gasp. We'd had a taste of spring, and returning to winter was dismal. The ground was well-covered and snow was still falling, the flakes large and so thick I felt I was seeing the landscape through a transparent dotted curtain. The tiny yellow jonquils, bold and vivid on Saturday, were pathetic Sunday morning, their golden petals drooping under the weight of the snow and their thin green foliage spraddled on the white earth.

When I opened my bedroom door I could smell bacon and the rich, mellow scent of fresh coffee coming from the direction of the kitchen. Voices murmured. Putting on a robe, I went downstairs to find Mama and Dad at the table.

"Christy, look at the weather!" My mother beamed. "Isn't it lovely? It's exactly what my garden needs, too. A hard rain would run off the land before it soaked in, but the snow is perfect."

I didn't think it was perfect. Far from it. "Some spring weather," I muttered and took my bacon from the oven where Mama left it to keep warm. "This is practically April and it's not fair to have another snow, especially when we're in a southern state like Virginia."

"Nobody can dictate to Mother Nature,"

Dad grinned. "As soon as it stops coming down I'll clear the walks and the drive but there's no point in starting yet."

It went without saying that I'd help Dad, and for once I didn't mind. It would be better to have something to do other than spending the entire day thinking of Mike.

All morning I dawdled around the house, taking twice as long as necessary to have a bath, shampoo my hair, and get into my clothes, wishing there was a more interesting activity planned for the afternoon than moving snow from one spot to another. If I hadn't already finished my school assignments I'd have studied that morning just to keep my mind busy, although on Saturday night I had been glad to do the homework as it gave me a reason to stay in my room and let me avoid Mama's questioning glances after Mike left. She'd given me every opportunity to mention him and tell her about the tractor ride, and I couldn't make myself do it.

On Sundays my family usually ate our big meal at midday instead of at night as we did during the week. That snowy Sunday she fixed veal chops with little potatoes browned in butter and green peas the way I liked them with mushrooms and herbs. I had the feeling she realized I was upset and in her way she was trying to make me feel better. But this was no simple hurt, not the sort she could kiss away as she'd done with bumps and scares when I was a small child. I ate, or tried to, swallowing a mouthful or two because she and Dad would have been concerned if I refused even though I might just as well have been chewing cardboard.

The snow stopped while I was drying the lunch dishes and Dad came stomping through the kitchen in boots and an old Navy pea jacket he always wore in what he termed "heavy weather." He'd served a hitch in the Navy when he was in his late teens, after his draft number was called, and a few sea-going expressions lingered in his vocabulary.

Some things which are fun when you're with a crowd or a friend seem dull if you do them by yourself, and to my way of thinking, anything in the snow fell into that category. Dad was out of sight down the hill, working on the steep part of the drive, and I started to clear the steps and walkways near the house.

I'd been working half an hour when my mother opened the window and said, "Telephone for you, Christy." Probably it was Betsy, I decided as I brushed snow from my boots and went in the kitchen door. After chemistry lab Friday, Betsy and I walked down the hall together and she'd commented that she didn't understand the assignment. "Maybe I'll give you a buzz and we can talk about it, Christy," she'd said as we separated to go to our next classes.

It wasn't Betsy who answered when I said, "Hello." Mike was on the line and hearing his voice made my knees wobble.

"I just thought I'd find out what you're doing," he said.

"Shoveling."

"Want some help?"

"I'd love it, Mike."

"Good enough. I'll be right over."

I caught my breath as I eased the telephone back into its cradle. *He was coming!* Mike Maxwell was actually coming to see *me*! I couldn't believe it. He wanted to see me again and he hadn't wasted a second telling me.

The day, which seemed drab until he called, was suddenly brimming with beauty. Snow was no longer merely white, but it sparkled, and the chill in the air was invigorating rather than just plain cold. Mike came in the jeep belonging to his uncle's service station, taking our hill effortlessly. He picked up Dad and the two of them were laughing about something as Mike stopped near me.

"I'll finish for you, Mr. Jamison," Mike said.

"That's an offer I can't turn down." Dad jumped lightly from the jeep and to my relief went in the house. I didn't want to have to talk to a boy in front of my parents because I knew I'd be tongue-tied with an audience. I might be tongue-tied regardless, but it would be worse with my father overhearing.

Mike and I looked at each other, both of us smiling. His skin was rosy from being in the open jeep and the black knitted cap was pulled over his ears, but I'd never seen anybody so handsome. His, "Hi, there," sent a lovely little shiver up my backbone.

"Hi, yourself," I said. "It's a big change from yesterday, isn't it?"

"Sure is. I asked your dad if he wanted me to clear the drive for him but he didn't think it was necessary since the jeep has made tire tracks. I'll do the walks, though. Even brought my own shovel in case your folks didn't have a spare."

That afternoon became a cameo in my mind, every incident carved clearly so I could treasure it, and the strange part is that while I know exactly how Mike looked, later I couldn't recall much of what we said while we were outside in the snow. I laughed often and so did he, and once I slipped on an icy spot, my hands waving wildly in the air, and he reached for my arm, grabbing it and saving me from going down. Despite his gloves and the thick fabric of my coat, my arm burned under his touch.

We made short work of the shoveling, and when it was finished built a fantastic snowman who resembled a person because he had legs rather than big round balls of snow for a body and feet.

"Name him, Christy," Mike said to me and I thought hard, finally announcing, "His name will be Melvin and by tomorrow he'll probably be known as Melvin, the Melted."

I suggested that we go in the house for something hot to drink, asking Mike if he wanted tea, coffee, or cocoa and making a mental note that he said he was "a nut about anything chocolate." Preparing two cups, I carried them from the stove to the kitchen table and apologized because we were out of marshmallows although Mike didn't mind. He stared at the mountains and commented that he'd always wondered how the bay windows looked from inside the house.

While we drank our cocoa I found out a little more about him: that his father worked for a farm equipment company and one of his older brothers was partner in a construction firm in Pennsylvania while the other was in the Marine Corps. His mother was a legal secretary over at the county seat ten miles from Greenview, and the few remarks he made about his home life indicated it was rather different from mine. He and his parents seldom did anything together and he added in an off-hand fashion that his mother didn't cook during weekends.

"You mean you eat out every Saturday and Sunday?" I asked. "Breakfast, too?"

"Oh, heck no. We each fix our own. My mother says she works hard five days a week beating the typewriter and does the house stuff at night so she wants Saturdays and Sundays free. Dad gets irked with her about it and sometimes he tells her she's not forced to have a job. But since she's not willing to cook, we snack rather than eat real meals on weekends. Lots of people do that these days, Christy. Jill's family — "

He broke the sentence off, his face very pink, and he promptly changed the subject by inquiring if I liked bay windows or was just tolerating them. My, "Yes. They're nice," had a far-off sound. I was dying to hear what he'd been on the verge of saying about Jill Rogers' family but I couldn't ask and he didn't bring it up again.

Outside, everything shimmered with a pearlish glow as the day began to fade. We'd long since finished our cocoa and still were on opposite sides of the kitchen table, the cups before us with faint brown stains in the bottom of each one. I thought that I ought to carry the cups over to the sink, maybe turning on the overhead light at the same time, but if I moved, the enchanted spell between us would be broken. My getting up might make Mike think I was hinting for him to leave.

After a while Mama came into the kitchen, flicking the electric switch so the room instantly became bright, and she invited Mike to have supper with us. "I'd better warn you," she added. "We've already eaten dinner in the middle of the day and tonight it's grilled cheese sandwiches and vegetable soup but the soup is homemade and there's plenty. Your staying for supper won't be any trouble."

"You've talked me into it, Mrs. Jamison, and you sure didn't have to twist my arm." He gave her the broad smile I'd come to love.

I knew my mother liked him or she wouldn't have offered such a warm supper invitation. She was always polite to my friends, but I could tell which ones she truly enjoyed.

It surprised me that Mike didn't ask to use

the phone to tell his family where he was. I'd have called if I wasn't coming home for a meal. His mother must not have expected it of him, as my mother did of me.

I set the table with a yellow flowered cloth which made a nice contrast to the blue pottery soup plates, and Mike propped himself against the wall, watching me and talking to Mama while she prepared the food. When she started to lift the heavy kettle of soup from the refrigerator to the stove he jumped forward and said, "Here, let me carry that for you, Mrs. Jamison." She asked what we wanted for dessert and Mike murmured that he ate everything. Remembering his fondness for chocolate, I mentioned having seen a box of brownie mix in one of the cabinets and Mike said quickly, "Man-oh-man-oh-man! I hit the jackpot tonight!" Mama, laughing at his exuberance, commented that she knew she was being smart Saturday afternoon when she shelled walnuts, as they could go in the brownies.

A little of my natural shyness returned when the four of us sat down to eat. I was afraid my mind would go blank since I wasn't accustomed to talking to a boy with Dad and Mama present, and the horrible fear nagged at me that Mike might slurp his soup or something, which would give him a black mark in Mama's eyes. I shouldn't have been concerned because his manners were fine and my parents saw to it that there were no long silences. While Mike and Dad were discussing the Greenview High baseball team, I let my eyes circle the room with its Dutch tiles and perky violet plant, glad we were in the kitchen instead of the dining room which was more formal.

"Christy, just stack the dishes and leave them tonight," Mama said as we got up from the table.

"You usually clean up after a meal?" Mike asked me. "I'll help. One thing I know how to do is wash dishes."

"Then you'd rather wash than wipe?"

He nodded and I almost told him we'd make a great team since I preferred drying, only I couldn't say that with Mama in the room.

It seemed to me that Mike and I laughed a lot in the kitchen, and after tidying up we joined my parents in the den to watch television. I'd have preferred our being somewhere by ourselves but I didn't know how to suggest it and I didn't want to ask him to stay in the kitchen, as though he wasn't good enough for the rest of the house. Our living room seemed as coldly formal to me as the dining room, and besides, the TV set was in the den.

It wasn't until Mike and I were going the short distance down the hall from the kitchen to the den that I thought about where we'd sit, and a small knot of panic rose into my chest. Our den was a tiny room with dark paneled walls and there was only space for a couple of tables, two chairs, and the sofa. Dad's favorite was the green striped easy chair which matched the ottoman, and Mama liked the low rocker. That left the sofa for Mike and me and I had the scary feeling it would be embarrassing if he sat close to me with my parents watching, and heartbreaking for him to be at the far end of the sofa with me way to the other end.

I sat down first, not quite in the middle but not jammed into a corner, either, and that forced Mike to take a corner. He chose the one furthest away, which put about eighteen inches between us, but we could have touched easily if we'd reached out to each other. We didn't, of course.

When a TV program ended at ten o'clock he mentioned not having done any homework for Monday but he didn't stand up or make a move to leave and I said, "Stay through the next show, Mike. It's only half an hour. You'll still have time to study." At ten-thirty he got to his feet and thanked Mama and Dad for supper, adding, "Mind if I use the back door? The jeep is parked in the backyard."

My mother's "Of course we don't mind, Mike" came with a smile. I went in the kitchen with him and didn't turn on the light, although we weren't in darkness as the hall light was burning. Mike put his boots and his jacket on, walking over to the door leading outside but making no effort to touch the knob, just standing there twirling the black knitted cap around and around on the fingers of his left hand.

"Christy, your folks are super," he said.

"They liked you, too."

"Do you like me, Christy?"

Don't you know? Can't you see? The question scorched my tongue but I settled for a lame-sounding, "You're really easy to like."

"Then you'll go out with me tomorrow night? There's a movie which is supposed to be good and — Hey, what's wrong? What did I do?"

"You didn't do anything." My voice was quivery although I hadn't realized my face reflected what was going through my mind. "It's just — just that I doubt if I can go anyplace on a school night. My parents are strict on that."

He continued to twirl the cap. My heart was in my throat.

"Well, what if I came over?" he asked.

"Oh, sure, Mike!"

"And you'll go out with me Friday?"

"Friday is wonderful."

His mouth curved into a smile. "We'll get together at school tomorrow, too. If you reach the cafeteria first, wait for me. Okay?"

I took a deep, slow breath, summoning all my courage to ask a question which had to be asked. I couldn't endure another scene similar to the one at Sonny's.

"Mike, if you and I eat lunch together at school tomorrow, won't that make Jill mad?" I seemed hoarse, almost as if I had a cold, and my pulse was so loud I marveled at his not hearing the thumping noise.

"Maybe so, but she can't give me orders," he answered snappishly. "Anyway, who cares if she's mad or not. That girl has a low boiling point and she can always find something to get angry about if she needs an excuse. Last night she — "

Until he hushed abruptly I wasn't aware of how rapidly I was breathing.

"Last night she did what, Mike?" I asked, surprised at my forthright question. I'd guessed when he drove off Saturday afternoon in the pickup that he had a date with Jill Rogers, but learning it positively came as a shock and now that we were talking openly about her, I wanted him to finish the sentence about what she had done.

"Look, Christy" — there was no mistaking the earnestness in his voice — "I had a whale of a lot of fun with you yesterday afternoon. Plowing the garden was work until you got on the tractor with me and we did it together and after that it was swell. Just plain swell. But — " He stopped twirling and put the cap on his head, rolling the edge up twice which meant scarcely more than the crown of his head was covered. "Christy, I already had a date lined up with Jill for last night and I figured there'd be fireworks if I didn't show, even though I'd rather have been with you. She and I had it out and she knows we're finished." He sucked his breath in, his eyes glued to my face. "You believe me, don't you? It's the truth."

"Yes, I believe you," I whispered and I don't know how it happened, but all of the sudden Mike had both of my hands in his, holding them very tightly.

At the moment something funny must have happened on the TV screen as Mama

112

and Dad burst out laughing. The unexpected sound startled us and Mike dropped my hands. "I'd better go now," he said. "See you tomorrow."

Standing by the bay window in the kitchen, I waved until he was out of sight over the snowy hill, all sorts of emotions stirring inside my body. It would be impossible for me to return to the den and continue staring at television, not with such happy turmoil rippling through me. I started upstairs, calling over the banister, "I guess I'll say good night," with music in my voice and hearing the answering, "Good night," from both Mama and Dad. My feet danced the rest of the way up, barely skimming the floor. I couldn't wait to be in my own room in the lovely silence where I could think about Mike as much as I pleased.

Chapter

· 10 ·

Monday began as such a perfect day I thought the good things would go on and on, and maybe I should have known better, but when you're truly happy, anything less seems unreal. During the morning and afternoon I was a different Christy Jamison. I became the girl who now had a boyfriend, the girl who felt beautiful because she knew she was liked — maybe even loved — by the most wonderful boy in the world. I moved in an exhilarated daze and I certainly didn't think that my mother, of all people, would end part of the rosy glow surrounding me. But she did it that evening.

Mike was waiting when I stepped off the bus at school Monday morning, leaning against the building with his coat collar turned up and his books lying in a stack on the pavement at his feet. He tucked his arm through mine as we went inside which was the way he'd walked with Jill unless he was holding her hand, and my breathing increased in tempo at the realization. We passed Betsy Collins in the hall and I saw her mouth drop open and her eyebrows go up.

"Last night I nearly offered to bring you to school today," Mike said. "But I've been known to oversleep in the mornings, especially if I leave all my homework until the last second as I did this past weekend, and I figured it wouldn't score any points with you if I made you late for classes just as we began dating."

"Oh, you're trying to score points with me?" I asked in a teasing way and laughed, amazed at how easy it was to flirt when a boy so obviously responded.

"Darned right. All the points I can make. I'll give you a ride home this afternoon on my way to work, though. That is, unless you'd rather ride the bus."

"I'd rather ride with you, Mike." As I spoke I felt the slight pressure of his arm against mine and when I glanced up at him, he was smiling at me. I wanted to laugh aloud from sheer joy.

My mind was filled with so many new thoughts I didn't pay much attention to classes that Monday, especially during math because the nearness of Mike sent an electric shock into my body. If he leaned forward I could feel his breath and he touched my hair, lifting it gently and rubbing his fingers across the back of my neck. The silly fear hit me that it would be terrible if my neck was dirty. It wasn't. I knew positively it wasn't. But if it should be and Mike saw a telltale smudge...

The worry was cut short when Mr. Hanson called on me. I heard him say, "Christy," but I hadn't heard another bit of the lesson and had no idea what the math discussion was about.

Instantly Mike's hand jerked away from my neck and with a very embarrassed face I said, "Would you please repeat the question, Mr. Hanson?" The students sitting near me weren't succeeding very well in hiding their smiles, and from the last row in the room, a boy snickered. Mr. Hanson's expression didn't change but his eyes bore into my eyes and I had the feeling he knew just as everybody else in class did that Mike Maxwell had been teasing me.

Following math I had chemistry lab and the instant that class was over Betsy bombarded me with questions. She and I shared a lab table and it was impossible to avoid her.

"I saw you and Mike this morning," she said. "That walking arm in arm bit — what does it mean, Christy? What's Jill going to say or do if she sees him with you *that way*, because she's Mike's girl?"

"I don't understand what you're talking

about when you say 'that way,' " I answered stiffly, knowing perfectly well what she meant.

"Come on, Christy! Don't play dumb. Are you dating him again? I know you went out with him once but have you been seeing him a lot since that night he brought you to Sonny's? Gosh, that was ages ago! I thought he'd been going with Jill exclusively all the time since."

There was a curious expectant look on her face but I wasn't ready to talk about Mike's and my relationship or about Jill. Not yet, anyway. I didn't want to admit even to myself that I wasn't completely sure what our relationship actually was. I knew what I wanted it to be, but I couldn't forget how high my hopes were after that first ride home until we went to Sonny's. If he dropped me again it would be awful enough, without my bragging in advance because he'd walked down the hall at school with me.

Ignoring Betsy's question, I said I needed to get a book from my locker before the next class, and I hurried away from her.

Mike and I were stared at constantly during lunch and I guess there were some whispered cracks and comments about us from the students at other tables. I pretended not to notice, although I felt very conspicuous. At Greenview High, especially in the cafeteria, watching the going-steady couples, and talking about who'd broken up with whom, and which girl was dating which boy, and vice versa was standard conversation. I felt self-conscious under the stares although if they bothered Mike or if he was aware of them, he didn't let it show.

Jill sat at a table across the cafeteria from us with a crowd of boys and two girls and it was impossible not to know she was in the room because of her bright hair and tinkling laughter, which sounded harsh to me that day. I tried to brace myself for her to join us, but she didn't. Mike had taken me to the table where Betsy and Gordon were sitting and they acted as though they didn't think it was out of the ordinary to find him with me.

By the time school closed for the day, Sunday's snow was melting under a blinding sun and small puddles of water glistened on the pavement. Patches of green showed through the white covering and as Mike drove me home we passed yards with crumbling snowmen. I asked Mike if he thought our Melvin really had become Melvin, the Melted and he flashed a grin without answering. Chatter was unnecessary with the radio in the car playing music. I was sitting in the middle of the car seat and it seemed very natural for Mike to be holding my hand. The little squeeze he gave my fingers when he stopped at my door made me tingle.

"I wish I didn't have to go to work," he said softly and it seemed to me there was a new tenderness in his smile. "But I do."

"Can't you come in for just a few minutes, Mike?"

"I'd better not. If I want my paycheck I

have to get to work on time. See you tonight, though."

"I'll be waiting. Do you know what time you'll come?"

"Eightish, I guess. You'll be finished with dinner by then, won't you?"

"Usually we start around six when Dad gets in, so I'm sure we'll be done long before eight. The dishes, too." I smiled. "You won't have to help with them."

I had to pull my hand from his and as he drove off I thought how much brighter everything seemed than it had Saturday afternoon when I was fighting tears as Mike took the jeep down the hill. Then, I'd been hurt, positive Mike didn't care a snap for me, and now I knew it wasn't that way at all.

Mama was in the den knitting and watching television. "You're early today, dear," she said. "The bus must have been ahead of schedule."

I had the feeling she knew I hadn't come on the bus but I let it pass. "Mike brought me." My tongue caressed his name although my voice felt strained but it didn't actually squeak as it had when I mentioned him to Mama earlier. That was the moment for me to add casually, if possible, that Mike would be over later, and I didn't do it, partly because I had a sneaking fear Mama might remind me it was a school night, and partly because I wasn't sure I could say anything else about Mike without baring the depths of emotion rippling over me.

To be doing something, I went in the kitchen for a snack. I wasn't hungry but eating after school was my routine and the rich smell of chocolate came full in my face as I took the lid off the tin cake box which held the brownies. Those brownies had "Mike" all over them in invisible letters and I knew just how he'd looked Sunday night when he tasted his first one and said, "Mmmmm, Mrs. Jamison. These are the most," and I also knew I didn't want a brownie unless Mike was having one, also. Carefully replacing the box lid, I poured a small glass of grapefruit juice from an opened carton in the refrigerator and made myself return to the den. Mama would have thought it strange if I hadn't joined her.

"Anything interesting happen at school today?" she asked as she had dozens of other afternoons. This was our routine, too. I took another sip of juice and claimed it was merely an "ordinary Monday" which had to be the understatement of the year.

"What did you do all morning?" I asked quickly to turn the conversation away from myself.

She mentioned errands, saying she'd taken two of Dad's suits to be dry cleaned, bought stamps, and stopped by the drugstore to see if a paperback book she'd seen advertised was available, and it wasn't. These were the kinds of activities she reported nearly every day and in the past they hadn't seemed boring, but now I wanted her to finish telling me so I could escape to my room and my own dreams, irked with myself for the feeling. I realized she was lonely and I'd been lonely enough before the last forty-eight hours to be sympathetic.

"By the way, Christy," she said. "Your father is going to the Town Council meeting tonight since re-zoning a tract of land near the plant is to be discussed. The meeting begins early — seven-thirty — and I think I'll go with him. You can come along, if you want. You might enjoy seeing democracy in action in a small town."

"I — uh — don't guess I will tonight," I murmured, pleading homework and marvelling at how beautifully everything in my life was developing. If Dad and Mama left early for the meeting, Mike and I'd have the house to ourselves for a while. Not that we'd do anything we wouldn't have done with my family at home, but we would be able to talk without an audience. It was simply nicer to be alone, just the two of us.

When my parents drove off shortly after seven I made a dash to the den to close the draw drapes, plump the cushions, and straighten the magazines on the table by the green striped chair, leaving only one lamp burning. The room was filled with a soft, muted light.

Upstairs, I changed the slacks and sweater I'd had on all day for my best mauve tweed skirt which I never wore to school and the long-sleeved white silk blouse with tiny pearl buttons which Aunt Doris had sent me as a Christmas gift and which I saved for special occasions. Waiting in the hall so I could see Mike driving up, I told myself I was calm and intended to stay that way, but the instant the car's headlights shone through the darkness my heart began to pound.

"You look great, Christy," he said as he came in. "Smell great, too. I like that perfume."

Both of us were smiling and I couldn't think of a clever reply so I whispered, "Thanks, Mike," and we sat down on the sofa. Everything was comfortable and cozy.

"Your folks upstairs?" Mike asked.

I said they were out and with a saucy grin he slid over nearer me and put his arm around my shoulders, his fingers playing a faint rat-a-tat drum beat on my upper arm. I tilted my face up to his the way I'd seen girls do when they were with boys they liked — and that was the moment my world fell apart.

I was so engrossed in Mike I hadn't heard any noises outside and apparently Mike hadn't, either, especially as the drapes were drawn, because he was as stunned as I was when the back door of the house burst open and Dad bellowed, "Christy! Where are you? Are you all right?"

Mike and I sprang apart, both of us jumping up. "Here. In the den," I managed.

Footsteps scurried toward us, running, Dad's heavy ones and Mama's heels clicking when she came across the vinyl floor in the kitchen, the sound disappearing as she stepped on the rug in the hall.

"What in the — " Dad began in a rough voice, his eyes searching my face, then Mike's, and coming back to mine. I'd never seen him so grimly angry, and to add to the strangeness, in his right fist he clutched a stick of firewood about three feet long and maybe three or four inches in diameter.

"I thought you were here alone, Christy!" he barked. "You told your mother you had to study and when we started up the hill and saw an unfamiliar car parked at the house, we didn't know if you were being attacked or robbed or what!" He waved the wood in the air. "I picked this up outside in case I needed a weapon."

I gasped, then choked. All of the oxygen seemed to have drained out of my lungs and when I opened my mouth, I couldn't speak.

Dad's breathing slowed almost to normal but anger remained in his face and my mother stood in one spot as though her feet were cemented to the rug, making no move to unbutton her coat as she glared at me and said coldly, "Christy, you didn't tell me you were planning to have company tonight *on a school night*. I thought you said you had a good deal of homework to do."

Mike got the message. He'd have had to be blind, deaf, and dumb not to know he was unwanted — at least, unwanted by my parents. "I have to study, too," he mumbled. "Don't bother to see me out, Christy. I know the way."

Sick with embarrassment, I was panicky. Mike moved so fast I had to run to reach him and he scooped his coat off a chair in the hall where I'd put it, not pausing to put it on. I tried to speak and didn't say anything, and as he yanked the front door the look on his face was unreadable.

After he left I stood in the hall a long minute, leaning against the door with the knob cutting into the small of my back. He might be gone for keeps. He might not consider me worth the effort and no boy could be expected to take up time with a girl if being with her was made unpleasant. A bitter taste came into my mouth. It wasn't fair to have this happen just as Mike was beginning to like me, and who could blame him now if he went back to Jill?

A reaction was setting in, making me ache, and it didn't help to know I had no choice about facing my parents. Mama and Dad had put Mike on the defensive without actually accusing him with words, and it was apparent they didn't trust me. Looking at my watch, I swallowed a sigh. It was seventeen minutes after eight which meant Mike and I were together less than twenty minutes, and my father was acting as if I'd spent the entire night with him.

Dad, standing at the window when I reached the den, had put the stick of wood on the hearth, and Mama was sitting very erect on the green striped chair, her coat still buttoned to her chin. Maybe she was freezing. I was on fire, waves of heat suffocating me as they spun around my head.

"We weren't doing anything wrong," I

blurted out. "We were just talking. Is that a crime? Why were you spying on us? I don't know why you're so angry now."

"We weren't spying, Christy." My mother's voice dripped ice. "Your father had the wrong night for the Town Council meeting. It's tomorrow, not tonight, and when we came home and saw that car here, we didn't know if you were being raped or were dead or what. I doubt if you realize how frightened we were for you."

"But did you have to be so crude and put on such a big display and embarrass me in front of Mike?" My anger was showing. "The way you glared at us was — "

"That's enough, Christy!" Dad cut in. "Your mother is not crude and you're not to speak to her in that tone again. Is that clear?"

The fight went out of me. I managed to nod, looking down at the toes of my shoes. Dad didn't understand, and my mother, who was usually eager for my happiness, was treating me as though I were a criminal when all I'd done was talk to a boy, a boy they knew and appeared to like.

"You must have known in advance that Mike was coming here or you wouldn't have changed clothes and dresesd up after we left the house," Mama went on. "Why didn't you say something to me about it? You aren't sneaky by nature, Christy, but that's the way you're acting tonight."

"It wasn't a real date. Mike merely said he'd come over for a little while." I jerked my chin up, facing her. "I'm not a ten-year-old, Mama. I'm sixteen now and I didn't think I had to report every time I brushed my teeth or combed my hair or saw a friend."

She ignored my sarcasm and continued in the same steely tone. "Didn't you deliberately fail to mention it because you were afraid I'd veto Mike's visit since this is a school night?"

I couldn't deny it, and I guess she and Dad knew that. My face burned, so hot it had to be blood red.

"Is that so awful?" I began, and the thin, whirring noise which was my voice failed. I didn't move or say more and I just stood there waiting for whatever punishment they wanted to hand out. They were lenient with me in most situations but this was not "most situations." I might be grounded after school for a long time or my TV privileges could be taken away or I might not be permitted to drive the car for days. Or weeks.

Please don't say I can't see Mike Friday — if he still wants to date me . . . please. The words were a prayer inside of me. It wasn't as though I was failing in school. I wasn't a brain but I knew how to study and my grades were A's and B's and I never had to be reminded to finish school papers or projects. Mama and Dad knew that just as they also knew I was aware of disobeying their stupid rule about what I did on school nights.

All of a sudden I felt as if I were choking. Everything bound me. My clothes were too snug, even my underwear. I waited, dying inside, until Mama said, "Go on and do your lessons, Christy. We'll talk about this later."

"Later" didn't settle anything and it only prolonged the agony of not knowing if they'd refuse to let me date Mike Friday night — *if* he wanted to see me. I couldn't avoid that *if* in my tortured thoughts.

Concentrating on homework was futile. I undressed, putting on my pajamas and a robe, curling up on the window seat with my chin resting on my knees. The wide vista visible through the bay window showed a lemony moon rising over the mountains, illuminating the glistening sprinkling of snow which remained on the slopes. If I hadn't been in such turmoil I might have thought the night was beautiful, but it seemed cold and forbidding like everything else in my world.

I knew I was going to cry. Tears boiled in my throat and I pressed my fingertips against my cheeks to try to make myself calm but it was no use and the tears rose and rose until they spilled from my eyes and rolled down my chin. Some girls cry over the least little problem but I'd never been that kind and I didn't sob loudly or moan or fling my hands around. The sobs were inside me, suffocating me, and they had to come out. After a little while they slowed and gradually stopped, but the hurt remained.

For a moment I considered telephoning Mike. Just hearing his voice would be a comfort. There was an extension phone in my parents' bedroom across the hall and if they were downstairs, I could contact Mike without their knowing.

But what would I say to him? I swallowed and the knot in my throat didn't go away. Pleading for him to forget the scene at my house was ridiculous. He wouldn't forget. Besides, I didn't think I could bear to hear him call off our Friday date. Not yet. Maybe, I thought wistfully, by morning I'd be strong enough to endure it. Or, by later in the week I'd be accustomed to the idea.

I was still sitting on the window seat when my mother knocked on the door and called, "Christy," softly at the same time, coming in without waiting for a reply. My head was turned slightly toward the window and I didn't move.

"Haven't you done any of your assignments for tomorrow?" she asked. There wasn't any criticism in her voice, just concern.

"I'll get to them eventually."

"Christy — "

The way she spoke my name with a ragged, haunting quality in her voice made me turn to look at her, and she was as miserable as I was, her eyes shadowed and a strained set to her lips. I wanted to say, "It's all right, Mama. I don't hate you," but I didn't do it. I didn't do anything.

"Christy, I think I owe you an apology. Owe Mike one, also," she said quietly. "Tonight when your father and I drove up to the house and saw that car, I was terrified. I've

129

never been that frightened in my life and I was sure that some awful hoodlum was attacking you — and so was your Daddy. When we came in I — I suppose I lost my senses."

She inhaled deeply and for the first time I noticed her hands were shaking. "You were wrong not to tell me in advance that Mike was coming over, Christy, and I was wrong to fuss with you in front of a guest. Your report cards are superior and you've never had a bad attitude about school, and I ought not to have made such a to-do about a boy being here on a school night, not when this is the only time it's happened."

"Oh, Mama . . ." I whispered, my voice breaking. We reached for one another at the same instant and I clung to her with the sensation that she also was clinging to me. The familiar feel of her shoulder against my cheek was wonderful and when we broke the embrace both of us were smiling in a trembly way with a mistiness in our eyes.

"Mama, I can't stand for you to be mad with me. I'm sorry about the way I acted tonight. I truly am."

She smoothed my hair away from my face, her hand soft on my forehead. There was something reassuring in my mother's touch. "I feel the same way," she said. "You and I've always had such a good relationship and now that it's growing into an adult relationship, I shudder at the idea of saying or doing something to upset it."

"Don't worry." I gave a low laugh. "You

and I have a mutual appreciation society going, Mama."

She laughed, too, and I relaxed as she sat down beside me on the window seat. The mood only lasted a second because she said, "Now, let's talk about the Mike situation," and every nerve in my body snapped. I went tense. All the talk about good relationships appeared to be a farce.

"Mike's been in evidence so much these last few days I'm sure he likes you as much as you do him," she went on, "and it's time to make some ground rules. If you care about him, you ought to consider that it's not just your school grades which will topple if you don't study regularly — and study enough — but Mike's will, too, and I know you don't want to be the cause of that. He works every afternoon and he can't, or shouldn't, run around every evening during the school year."

What she said made sense although I'd never thought along those lines before.

"Weekends are a completely different situation." Mama's light tone was underlaced with seriousness. "That's the time for you two to have fun together and date."

"I promise I won't let him come here on school nights unless I ask you about it first. Mike — " A tremulous sigh tore from me. I wasn't kidding anybody but myself. There wasn't much reason to think I'd be seeing a lot of Mike Maxwell in the future. "Mama, I — you — you shouldn't give it a second thought," I muttered. "Mike might not want to come back."

"Because of what happened tonight? Oh, I hope not!"

"He — he didn't say anything when he left." My voice quivered. "He's already mentioned our doing something this coming Friday night, but now . . . I'm not sure. . . . I-I guess I shouldn't count on it."

Because I didn't want her to see the despair which had to be showing in my face, I turned my head toward the window. The moon was paler, higher in the sky, and it shone through the bare tree branches to put a latticed pattern of black lines on the ground in the yard. I fixed my eyes on the distant mountains, not actually seeing them, blinking to stop the tears which were clinging to my lashes.

"Would it help if I spoke to Mike?" she asked. "I could drop by the service station tomorrow afternoon after he gets to work and apologize — "

"*No!* Please don't, Mama! Please!"

"All right, I won't if you'd rather not. I just thought it might ease the situation if I let him know I hope he'll continue to come here. I wouldn't say anything else."

I shook my head. She was trying to help. I realized that, but this was between Mike and me, and whether or not he still wanted to see me was up to him.

My mother stood up and leaned over to kiss me on the forehead. "You'll feel better if you put your mind on something else, dear," she said. "Try to study a little. Everything will seem better in the morning."

Nothing was better Tuesday morning. After Mama went out of my room Monday night, studying was a joke. I flipped through the pages of one text and never bothered opening the others.

I had a hard time getting to sleep and it seemed to me I woke up every ten minutes all night long, so cold I'd pull up the extra blanket from the foot of the bed, or so hot I'd kick all the covers off. I dreamed endless, unsettling dreams without remembering anything once my eyes were open except that Mike had been in those muddled reveries.

The rough night showed in my face Tuesday morning and makeup didn't do much to help the dark circles under my eyes. What difference did it make how I looked, I thought mournfully as I started downstairs to breakfast. Mike probably would stay so far from me he wouldn't know whether I was all right or not.

Mama and Dad already were at the table, my mother wearing her red housecoat and chattering in such an animated way it was obvious she was trying to pretend nothing had happened, and neither Mike nor the events of the previous night were mentioned. For a miracle my parents failed to comment on my not eating. Usually breakfast was one of my favorite meals, but that morning I pushed the scrambled eggs around on my plate with a fork and broke a slice of toast into mouthful-sized bits, but when I tried to chew one, it expanded and expanded on my tongue until finally I gulped and swallowed just to be rid of the soggy mass.

On the school bus I deliberately chose the vacant seat beside a girl I barely knew named Millie Cameron, because she was studying like mad, her looseleaf notebook propped open on her knees while she worked on some sort of graph with a red ballpoint pen and a ruler. That meant I didn't have to talk, and I wanted the time to plan how to greet Mike.

I'd be casual, as casual as possible, I decided. If he made it apparent he was finished with me, I wouldn't let him — or anybody — know I was hurt. At least, I'd try to hide my feelings. I'd be aloof, just the way he was the Monday after our trip to Sonny's, and I'd think up some funny, brittle crack to toss out in case Betsy or anybody else asked why Mike and I weren't together in the cafeteria after being such a close twosome there at noon the previous day. Maybe I wouldn't bother going to the cafeteria at all. I could find an empty classroom and use the hour to study. Besides, I doubted if I'd be able to eat.

When the bus turned from the street into the school grounds I wanted to appear as though I didn't have a care in the world and I made a big effort to smile, my lips so stiff my mouth felt pulled until that so-called smile must have resembled a jack-o'-lantern.

Don't let Mike be with Jill. Don't let him be holding her hand. The silent words gripped me and the Halloween smile froze on my face. I shut my eyes, but I had to open them when the bus stopped and the other students filled the aisle, elbowing their way out.

I saw Mike immediately.

He was standing in exactly the same spot where he'd been Monday morning, lounging against the corner of the building, only this time he had his books under one arm rather than at his feet and as I stepped down from the bus to the pavement he started toward me, running.

"Hi, there," he said, his eyes on mine. There was no anger in his face, just concern and caring.

"Hi, yourself," I managed from deep in my throat and realized I had my own smile once more, not the fake one.

"Christy, can we talk a sec before school starts? There's a bunch of stuff I want to say and — well — " He jerked his head at the throng of students milling around the unloading area. "Too many people are here."

I must have answered yes or nodded because he took my hand and we hurried past the building and across the parking lot to his car. I got in first and he didn't go to the driver's side, but slid in after me, the warmth of his body seeping into mine, and when I turned my head to look at him in the morning sunlight, I could see the tiny pores in his skin. His shirt was open at the neck and the faint bulge of his Adam's apple showed in his throat.

"About last night . . ." He sucked his breath in.

"Mike, I don't even want to mention about last night if you're not mad."

"Did you catch hell after I left? Your folks were plenty uptight when they came home."

"It was a misunderstanding. Everything is fine now. Honest."

The doubting look stayed in his eyes although his mouth softened and he lifted his left arm, putting it around my shoulders. I sat very still, loving the feel of it across my back, wishing he'd also do the same with his right arm and lock me in an embrace. It didn't happen, and in the next moment I was thankful he kept that right hand in his lap as I realized how public the parking lot was.

"At first when your parents started carrying on I felt like I was in the way and ought to go on the double," he said. "But then, after I saw how you looked when you came to the front door with me, so scared, I wondered if you thought I was being chicken and barging out to leave you to take full blame for whatever we did that had your mom and dad so steamed up."

"I didn't think that about you, Mike. You didn't do anything wrong, either. My parents know it now." I gave a faint, nervous smile. "My mother even wanted to come by the service station this afternoon and apologize to you, but I told her not to."

"Score one for you. I'd have been embarrassed if she had."

He was due an explanation and I floundered for the right words. "It's just — just that in the past I've always told Mama or Dad if I had any plans, and last night — well, I didn't. I didn't say you were coming. Since last night was a school night and they take a dim view of my doing anything except studying on school nights, they really were scared when they saw your car and didn't know whose it was. They thought it belonged to a burglar who was inside the house."

I couldn't say "rapist," instead of burglar, but Mike knew.

"No wonder they blew up," he said. "Gosh, Christy, I don't wonder your dad came barging in, yelling and waving that hunk of wood. What if it really had been some goon hurting you?" His voice became firm and hard. "That hill where you live is so isolated and from now on if you're in the house alone, especially after dark, you lock up good and don't open a door to anyone you don't recognize. Okay?"

He was concerned about me. The realization gave me a delicious feeling.

"I promise," I murmured. "I almost telephoned you last night. But I was afraid you wouldn't want anything else to do with me."

"Whatever gave you the stupid idea I'd stopped liking you, Christy? Know something wild? I almost called you, too. But I figured with my luck your mom or dad would answer and — "

He was interrupted by the first school bell. That meant we had two minutes to get from the car, across the parking lot to the building, and into our homerooms if we didn't want to be counted late. At Greenview High any student with three late slips and no excuse had to stay one hour in study hall after classes for an entire week. We got out of the car and broke into a run. Mike could have out-distanced me easily as his legs were so much longer than mine, but he grabbed my hand and kept a stride I could follow although I was panting.

"See you at lunch," he called as we separated.

He went down the long corridor and I started up the stairs. The halls were nearly deserted with only a few stragglers in sight, all of them moving fast. The final bell jangled just as I reached Mrs. Perkins' room and sank into my chair.

Chapter

· 11 ·

During a lull in the conversation at lunch Friday, Mike asked what I'd like to do that night.

"Go to Sonny's," I came back promptly, and to my consternation, all the boys at our end of the cafeteria table laughed.

Bud Warren, who was sitting on the other side of Mike, said in a sardonic tone, "Ask a simple question and you'll get a simple answer, fella. Why didn't you just go on and find out right now if she wants to go to Lookout Knob?"

Everybody laughed again and I could feel my forehead turning pink. Lookout Knob was an isolated spot on one of the mountain roads and it was accepted that if a couple went there, it was for more than kisses.

Bud and Mike lived on the same street and

had been friends all of their lives, I'd already discovered. Bud was a likeable boy, easy to get along with and with a nice sense of humor, which was fortunate as he was painfully homely, as ugly as Mike was handsome in my estimation. Like Mike he was tall, with a similarly sturdy body, but Bud's head was tiny, out of proportion to the rest of him, and his ears stuck straight out on either side of his face like pitcher handles. His mouth was too wide and his pale eyes were dwarfed by bushy straw-colored eyebrows which seemed out of place with his dark brown hair.

"Christy, do you have that firm an opinion about everything?" Gordon asked me from across the table as the laughter died following Bud's crack about Lookout Knob. "You didn't even catch your breath between Mike's question and your answer."

"Knock it off, you guys." Betsy glanced first at Gordon and then let her gaze include all the boys. "Don't mind these creeps, Christy. They can be rude, crude, and gross at times."

"Sure, we can. But you love me anyway, don't you?" Gordon grinned in her direction before leaning over to nuzzle her cheek with his chin. She obviously wasn't irked but she did look rather flustered, as Mr. Brady, the principal, was eating his lunch across the cafeteria and there were rules about students kissing in the building or on the grounds.

The others at the table must have expected me to give Mike a vague answer, but

none of the students at Greenview High —
not even Mike — realized I'd had practically
no experience talking to boys until that week.
They could never guess how I'd longed to
return to Sonny's ever since the first time
Mike took me there because it was the spot
where everybody gathered and I wanted to
be included in the fun, to see the crowd as
well as to let them see I was dating.

Those were the things I couldn't say aloud
just as I'd have died if I'd had to admit how
unsure of myself I continued to feel around
boys, even around Mike. Some girls seemed
to be born knowing automatically how to
flirt and keep a conversation going and what
to say, but I wasn't one of them.

Apparently it had become general knowledge at school that Mike and I were dating,
even though probably no one realized we
hadn't been able to have real dates yet. I
knew my status was improved since I'd been
seen with him in the halls or getting into his
car at the close of classes. Girls who formerly
didn't bother to take up time with me or who
settled for a terse hello if I spoke first now
chatted a little, and on Thursday afternoon
Betsy phoned the house just to gab, something she hadn't done before. The two or
three times she'd called me previously were
for the definite purpose of asking about a
homework assignment and she'd hung up
quickly.

I dared not think of myself as "Mike's
girl" which was how Jill had been known.
Yet, there were little signs which made me

aware I was no longer merely "that girl who moved here from up north." All of it struck me as odd. I was the same. I felt the same and couldn't find anything different in my behavior or the way I looked even though I had to admit my eyes sparkled more in the last three days.

I certainly didn't treat people at school differently from the way I'd been doing since January, but having a boy notice me raised me to a higher level among the kids, especially when that boy was Mike Maxwell, who was generally liked. In the short space of one week with Mike spending time with me, I'd become Somebody with a capital S at Greenview High.

When Mike and I were leaving the cafeteria that Friday I said, "If you have other plans for tonight, we don't have to go to Sonny's. It's all right with me if you'd rather not. I simply said the first thing I thought about."

"Sonny's is fine with me." He shifted his books from his left arm to his right and cleared his throat. "Look, Christy, don't let what happened a few minutes ago get you down. I saw you blushing when the gang laughed."

Instantly my face was hot again. "I wish I didn't blush! It's so awkward."

"I like it. So, don't stop. Okay?"

He smiled and I felt fluttery all over.

"The fellows were just teasing you and they didn't mean any harm," he went on.

"Especially Bud. He goes out of his way not to hurt people or say rough stuff because he's had to endure a lot of ugly remarks about his ears and he knows what it's like to be on the receiving end."

"It doesn't matter, Mike." It *did* matter, but I didn't want him to know.

"Right now Bud's down on females. All females, I guess. It's because of Jill."

My mouth went dry. This was the first time Mike had mentioned Jill Rogers to me since the previous Sunday at my house. I didn't want him to talk about her at all since that would put her in his thoughts, but my curiosity was getting the best of me.

"What about Bud and Jill?" I asked, the words rolling on my tongue like small, round marbles.

"Bud's always had a thing for her, ever since we were in grammar school. Would you believe he sent her fifty valentines the year we were in the fifth grade? Fifty! He'd been saving money for weeks to buy them and Mrs. Rutherford, the teacher, got mad as the devil when the valentine box was opened and practically every other one had Jill's name on it." Mike shook his head at the memory. "Jill never spends time with Bud unless she's real free, meaning that she doesn't happen to have some other guy wrapped around her little finger at the moment. When she and I called it quits, Bud sort of expected to step in."

"And he hasn't?" My voice was thin.

"She called him last Sunday and let him take her to the movies Sunday night, and I heard they were together at Sonny's Monday and Tuesday and Wednesday nights, but since then she's given him the ice-water treatment in a heap big way because she has her sights set on Vince Halloran."

We stopped near the stairs. In a few minutes when the bell rang, Mike would go to the second floor for English while I headed for history. I waited for him to tell me something about the boy Jill hoped to date, wanting to know and at the same time, dreading to discuss her, and when Mike kept quiet I said, "Who is Vince Halloran?"

"He quit school last fall. He was a senior but never opened a book and was flunking which is why he dropped out as I guess he knew he wouldn't graduate in June. His married sister lives in Ohio and he went out there to work in November, but he came back to town last weekend. I haven't seen him although Gordon has, and he said Vince is trying to find a job here." Mike's mouth twisted ever so slightly and he added, "Vince dated Jill in the past. Well, hasn't everybody, for that matter?"

It wasn't a question to demand an answer but I was surprised at the caustic quality in his voice, something I'd never heard before. Mike went on in the same slightly sneering tone, which wasn't like him. "Didn't you notice that Jill wasn't in the cafeteria today, Christy? I'll bet any amount of money she

144

sneaked off with Vince to a drive-in restaurant for lunch."

Strange, nagging thoughts were forming in my mind, thoughts I longed to push aside and couldn't. Had Jill given Mike the ice-water treatment, to use his phrase, when Vince Halloran returned to Greenview from Ohio? Was Vince's arrival what Mike and Jill argued about the Saturday night after he plowed my mother's garden with the tractor? Was that what actually broke Mike up with Jill, because she preferred being with her former boy friend, and was that the real reason Mike came to my house in the snow Sunday afternoon, since he didn't have anything more interesting to do? If Vince couldn't find a job he liked in Greenview or if he left town again for whatever reason, would Mike drop me and hurry back to Jill once more?

My head was whirling. To steady myself I fixed my gaze on a crumpled candy wrapper which some student had dropped on the school stairs, horrified that the wad of paper seemed to be dancing up and down. I knew it hadn't moved. My vision was blurred from the sudden mist in my eyes.

"Christy, are you okay?" Mike's voice jarred me away from my thoughts. "You look sort of strange."

Digging my nails into the palms of my hands, I forced a smile and assured him I'd never felt better. At the same moment, I made up my mind not to dwell on the fright-

ening questions about Mike and Jill and why
he no longer dated her. Mike was with me at
the moment, I reminded myself, and that was
the important part.

Mama's car was parked at our back steps
and she was unloading groceries when Mike
drove me up our hill after school that afternoon.

"Wait, Mrs. Jamison," he called to her.
"I'll carry those things in for you."

"Thanks, Mike, but I have only one
more," she said and picked up the brown-
paper bag from the backseat, handling it so
easily it had to be filled with light items. This
was the first conversation between my
mother and Mike since Monday evening and
I was thankful both of them sounded casual
as though there never had been an unfortu-
nate episode.

Mama went in the house, and I opened the
door of Mike's car, hating to get out and
knowing it must be done immediately so he
could make the service station on time. We
smiled at each other and I said, "See you
tonight," which wasn't nearly as personal
as I meant to be. It was such a lame remark
when I'd been waiting all week — all my life
— for Friday night.

His "Right on, Christy" echoed in my ears
as he sped off and it seemed to me I was forever watching Mike drive down our hill.

The afternoon was so pleasant I didn't go
straight indoors. Strolling over to the big

rocks in the backyard, I took a seat on the stone bench and thought all days should be as lovely as that one, neither hot nor cold but comfortably in-between. I felt good sitting there in the April sunshine. Pale green fuzz showed on several trees and the grass had a bounce to it rather than the wintry dryness which made every footstep a crunch. A few tiny yellow flowers were open on the graceful forsythia bushes which grew in a thicket at the rear of the yard and despite the snow and cold snap killing the jonquil blooms, their slender, dark-green foliage was standing erect once more.

My eyes moved from the blue sky to the bluer mountains to the plowed garden, and perhaps it was my imagination but I thought I got a whiff of the rich earthy odor from the soil. The garden land looked very black in contrast to the small white envelopes with colorful pictures which once contained seeds and which Mama had stuck on short sticks in the furrows to mark her plantings. Orange-hued carrots were on one envelope and red, red radishes on another. The picture of lettuce was a vibrant green and I wondered vaguely how long we'd have to wait before we had a truly fresh salad from our own backyard.

All of it made me remember the fun Mike and I had on the tractor. Closing my eyes, I knew just how he looked when he motioned for me to take a seat between his legs and how my back felt rubbing against his chest and the way he'd laughed deep in his body when he yelled, "Hang on, Christy," and made a U-turn, his arms tight against my ribs to keep me from tumbling off. The memories were delicious. I went over and over them in my mind, relishing every one.

I must have been on the stone bench fifteen or twenty minutes when something made me glance at the house. I felt I was being watched, and as I looked in that direction my mother was standing at the back door with the strangest expression on her face. She'd been staring at me, I suppose, and when I became aware of it and met her eyes across the yard, she whirled around and disappeared. That wasn't like her. I expected her to call out some casual remark in her cheerful voice, and when she didn't the silence seemed much louder than any noise would have been. I jumped up and went indoors at once.

The mess in the kitchen made me catch my breath. Usually everything was in place, exactly where it was supposed to be as Mama loathed unnecessary clutter, but that afternoon our kitchen looked the way it always did on moving day. The counters and table were covered with jars, cans, packages, boxes of food and brown paper bags, some still full and some already empty, the empty bags lying at crazy angles on the floor. All the cabinet doors stood wide open.

"I didn't realize we'd been hit by a tornado," I said.

Mama, who was putting eggs, oleo, and

cheese into the refrigerator, gave a small laugh. "It does look that bad, doesn't it? We were out of everything — staples, canned goods, soap — everything. I've just spent a fortune at the grocery store and now there's the ordeal of trying to find room for all of it, but with luck I won't have to shop again for a couple of weeks except to buy milk and fresh fruit. The past few days the weather has been so nice I've been more interested in working outdoors than in keeping up with supplies in the house."

I picked up a roll of paper towels and a box of tea bags, fitting them on their respective shelves, doing the same with several cans of vegetables and a cardboard box of paper napkins.

My mother didn't talk, which seemed odd, and she went about her work in an almost eerie quiet. Surely she will say something in a minute, I thought, and when she didn't I wondered if she could be angry with me. She'd have told me if that was the case, I felt positive. Since Monday night I couldn't recall anything I'd done which would upset her enough to make her clam up so completely, and I hadn't neglected my household chores. At least, I didn't think I had neglected anything.

Since Monday night . . .

A prickly sensation made my tongue burn. In robot fashion I continued to put cans in the cabinets and it dawned on me my mother and I hadn't talked, really talked, that is, since Monday night when she came to my room and apologized. After school Tuesday afternoon I'd said as little as possible to her and dashed upstairs to be by myself and daydream about Mike, and the same was true of Wednesday and Thursday afternoons, although on both of those last two days Mama had been in her garden when I came in from school.

Each time she was on her knees planting and she'd straightened up at the sound of the car, waving to Mike and me. On both days I'd gone straight in the house instead of walking down to the garden after Mike drove off. He'd told me if there was a lull at the gas pumps he'd phone, warning me not to be upset if he had to hang up in the middle of a word when a customer arrived. On Wednesday and Thursday afternoons I'd made a point of staying near the telephone, and it was heaven when he actually did call.

Late those two afternoons Mama came in just in time to have a quick bath and start making dinner before Dad arrived, and even though I'd helped her by setting the table and peeling potatoes or doing whatever she needed done, we'd said very little. It hadn't crossed my thoughts until she and I were in the midst of putting the groceries away in full silence to wonder what was on her mind, because until that moment I'd been too preoccupied with my own thoughts of Mike to care about much else. Now, though, the strain of the quietness was awful, a barricade between my mother and me.

"Mama — " My voice had a ragged sound.

"Yes, dear?"

"Mama, are you mad with me?"

"For heaven's sake, Christy! Of course I'm not mad with you. Whatever gave you such an idea?"

"I don't know. It's just — just — I don't know what it is, Mama." The words I was holding back began to tumble out in a gush. "I don't feel right. I'm not getting sick or anything — it's not physical. But — But I have to know if you're still irked because Mike was here Monday night or if you're angry at his bringing me home afternoons rather than my riding the bus. I can't think of what else it could be, but something is wrong between us. Between you and me. You're never this silent unless you feel terrible with a cold or a headache or — or if I've done something to upset you and right now, I don't know what it is I've done."

She'd been standing by the sink and she came across the kitchen, stopping in front of me. "Christy, you haven't done anything," she said.

"Then what — ?"

"Hasn't it occurred to you there've been some changes in your life in the last week, dear? I'm very glad you've become friends with Mike Maxwell and as to his driving you home after school, I certainly have no objection to that if you and he want it."

"This week . . . I've shut you out, haven't I?" I asked softly.

Not once had I mentioned Mike to her, or told her how he and I ate lunch together, or that every morning since Monday he'd been standing by the corner of the building, waiting for me. If those things had happened with a girl instead of a boy, I'd have gone into details relating all of it to my mother. Why hadn't I done the same thing about Mike?

I didn't realize how much she understood until she spoke again.

"You and I have always been close, Christy, and I hope we can continue that, but I also know there comes a time when teenagers — oh, how can I phrase it? When teenagers grow away from their parents. After a while they pick up the close relationship once again. That's how it was when I was your age. I went through a period of actually resenting my mother and father because they asked me so many questions about my friends and what I was doing that I was sure they couldn't possibly trust me. I thought they were crowding me, trying to dictate everything I said and did."

I picked up a jar of pickle relish, pulling at the label with the tip of my fingernail. "Did you get over feeling that way toward them?"

"Of course I did. It took years, though, and I made up my mind when you were born that I'd never do that to you. If I haven't already taught you right from wrong, it's rather late to begin now, so I'm counting on you to keep your common sense when you're with Mike. Only . . . only last Monday night I suppose I did the very thing I'd vowed not to do. As soon as your daddy and I realized you weren't in danger, I should have hushed — and I didn't."

"Last Monday night was a mistake for all of us, Mama. Please don't judge anything by that."

She sat down on one of the chairs by the table in the bay window. The late afternoon sunshine was blinding, coming in a white-yellow zigzag streak across the tabletop and she reached up to close the louvered shutter and cut the glare. I loved her so much it hurt and I wanted to tell her what was in my heart, and wasn't sure I knew how to express all of it.

"Christy, nothing has really changed between you and me. I'm right here if you need or want me, and so is your father, and I'd love to hear about Mike and your other friends. It's simply that I don't want to demand an outline of every thought you have." She paused, moistening her lips with the edge of her tongue and smiling a little. "I'm trying to convince myself you're getting to be an adult and it's time for this to happen, but if you want to know, I've missed you terribly this week."

"Oh, Mama . . ." We clasped hands across the table. I felt like laughing and crying at the very same moment and I think she did, too, as her eyes were shiny and her lower lip trembled ever so slightly despite her smile.

"Mike really is tops," I said, surprised that I wasn't embarrassed to speak his name to her.

"He certainly seems to be."

"Tonight we're going to Sonny's. That's okay with you, isn't it?"

She answered yes, speaking in her cheery voice at last. "He must be tops if you like him," she added. "It's obvious to me he has excellent taste if he wants to be with you."

Giggling, I told her that her prejudices were showing and with a laugh, she agreed. It felt great to be back on a familiar footing with her and to realize that just because I'd found a boy friend, I hadn't lost a mother.

Chapter

· 12 ·

Sonny's was bustling with noise and activity when Mike and I arrived that Friday night, the jukebox going full blast amid the rumble of voices and laughter. Several boys without dates sat on high stools at the soda fountain and beyond the arch with its plastic vines, the back room looked crowded. Every seat in the front section was taken except for the second booth where Bud Warren was on one side of the table with Betsy and Gordon across from him. Mike headed there at once.

The gleeful thought hit me that with five people in the booth, which originally was designed for four, there wouldn't be space for Jill Rogers and her date if they came in and wanted to join our group. She'd spoiled my evening once and even though the situation with Mike and me was different from that other Friday at Sonny's, I didn't want her to upset everything again. The truth, I realized ruefully, was that I wasn't at ease with her. Her beauty and self-assurance unnerved me, and when she was in sight I couldn't forget how much she and Mike meant to each other until recently.

The old drugstore booths at Sonny's were outdated with their tall-backed wooden seats painted a rusty brown and the rectangular tables topped with what looked like marble, the white stone flecked with veins of gray and all of it covered with scratched initials and scribblings. Despite the fact that the surface was too hard for carving with a knife the way wood would have held the letters, determined students had discovered that filling deep scratches with a ballpoint pen served the same purpose. As Mike and I sat down I hastily scanned the table for any familiar initials, especially for "M.M." and "J.R." but didn't find them.

"What's new with you, Bud?" Mike asked.

Bud looked glum, his protruding ears all the more noticeable, with his head leaning against the back of the brown seat. I felt sorry for him when his mouth twisted and he said, "Let's see, what's new. I made my first million today and got ninety-nine patents for a car engine that runs on soapsuds instead of gasoline. I believe that's all for the moment unless you count a big fat F on a history quiz."

"But, why don't you ask some girl for a date?" Betsy demanded. "You don't have to be nuts about the girl, but the sooner you get Jill out of your system — ''

The words were scarcely spoken when I saw Jill come in, walking with a stranger who was movie-star handsome. He had jet-black hair and a lean, square face with a cleft in the middle of his chin. They stopped at our booth as Mike got up to get us some hamburgers. Jill, her auburn hair gleaming like polished copper, took immediate command. In her breeziest manner she introduced Vince Halloran to me, quickly adding before I could speak, "I think there's room enough for everybody in the booth if we scrunch up. Mind moving to your right, Christy? All the way to the wall."

I minded, but I slid over and she and Vince sat down beside me, while Bud and Gordon inched in on the other side with Betsy. That left Mike standing and he scowled but didn't protest. Every now and then he'd shift his weight from one foot to the other or lean against the side of the booth and I could feel his eyes on me as I tried to drink my Coke. Vince was in the middle between Jill and me, and when he asked how I liked living in Greenview I knew somebody must have explained about my moving during January. I told him I liked it fine. The others talked which made me aware of my own silence, and of Mike's. I'd never known Mike to be quiet for so long.

Twice Vince mentioned leaving but Jill didn't move and after about twenty minutes he said, "Jill, Mike's going to be having leg cramps from standing there so long if we don't give him his seat."

"Oh, the poor darling," Jill cooed, but she got up.

Mike said, "See you, Vince," and as he sat down by me I was glad he hadn't said anything directly to Jill, not even good-bye. In her shoes I'd have felt snubbed at being ignored, but if she had the feeling, she kept it hidden.

"Of all the colossal nerve!" Betsy spluttered. "Why didn't you tell them to get lost, Mike? Or at least why didn't you ask to have your seat?"

"I don't own this property. They can sit wherever they want." Mike shrugged and gave a grunting snort. "I wasn't in the frame of mind for a bad scene, but if they'd hung around much longer I was going to see if Christy would mind going."

"Yeah, I was ready to head out, too," Gordon said. "You were smart to stay cool, Mike. Vince gets a bang out of throwing his weight around if he has an audience. Maybe he and Jill are made for each other. It doesn't take much to get either of them riled up."

Bud cleared his throat without uttering a word. I'd almost forgotten he was with us and it was embarrassing to look at him. I didn't know how deep his feelings for Jill ran, but it must have been awful for him to watch her with someone else. I hadn't forgotten the pain of seeing Mike with Jill, and that was when I scarcely knew Mike except to say hello. Mike turned to me. "Christy, I know you wanted to come here tonight and that's why we're still here."

"I'm ready to leave whenever you are," I said softly, and meant it. Going to Sonny's seemed ideal for everybody else, but my mood, which had been joyous earlier, had changed and I felt as bleak and disappointed as Bud looked.

It was just ten o'clock. Outside, the night was black without any stars, although a pale circle in the clouds glowed where the moon was attempting to break through and the air felt cold to my face. Mike walked with such a determined stride I had the feeling he might have forgotten I was with him, especially since neither of us spoke until we were in the car. It seemed ironic that Jill had spoiled another evening for us.

Mike put the car key into the ignition and without starting the motor he stretched both of his arms up, resting his palms flat on the ceiling. Sitting very still, scarcely breathing, I waited and finally he gave an aching sigh and said, "I'm sorry, Christy. I wanted everything to be perfect tonight and it's been a terrible evening."

"It wasn't your fault. You couldn't help Jill and Vince horning in." I'd said her name! I'd actually said it aloud and my mouth should have been as puckered as if I'd bitten into a green apple, only it wasn't.

Mike turned on the dashboard light and looked at his watch. "Too late for a movie," he said. "So, what would you like to do?"

"I don't care. Whatever you want."

"Whatever *I* want — Wow!" He grinned and there was a lilt in his voice. "You let yourself wide open with that answer. I don't even think I have the guts to tell you what I want."

His voice let me know he was the familiar Mike again, though. Lighthearted and smiling. That was what made me feel better.

"Maybe we'll drop the subject," I came back and forced a laugh. "We can go to my house."

The suggestion sounded prim, almost stuffy, and I wished I'd waited for him to decide what we'd do. Apparently Mike didn't mind as that's where we went, and the moment he turned from the highway into our drive I began to have doubts.

I didn't want us to have to be in the den with Mama and Dad, and I certainly wouldn't ask them to go somewhere else. It would be awkward if I led Mike into the living room with its formal atmosphere as both of us would be stiff and Mike wouldn't linger — and I wanted him to stay. The kitchen was all right except that it had no sofa, not even a bench. We'd be in separate chairs, probably at the table, and instead of the coziness of a booth such as the one at Sonny's, we'd feel as impersonal as if we were in an airport waiting room. I wanted to sit beside Mike, to touch him, and I didn't want my family for an audience. Not that we would do anything wrong. I knew we wouldn't. But I wanted privacy just the same.

It's uncanny how things work out. Instead

of stopping at the front where the porch light was burning, Mike drove around the house to the back and braked near the steps. The moon had come from behind the clouds and was making puddles of light and shadow on the ground, and as he cut the car engine there was a hush surrounding us.

"I guess your mother has her garden planted," Mike said, his tone unexpectedly soft.

"Part of it. Some of the early vegetables."

I almost added that it was too soon to put flower seeds in the ground as we might have another freeze, and then it dawned on me that Mike couldn't have cared less about that garden.

"Want to walk down there and see what's growing, Christy?"

A warm pulsing started in my throat as we got out of the car and Mike's arm went around my back as naturally as if he'd been putting it there forever. His hand rested on my waist, a feathery touch, and somehow his other hand found one of mine and held it, his fingers firm and smooth against my skin. We walked slowly and I wanted to look at him but turning my head even the tiniest bit might have marred the exquisite mood between us so I deliberately kept both eyes straight in front.

The mountains made a rich blue border across the distant horizon. I was conscious of the muted quiet. Not a single night bird chirped and insects make their noises in hot weather, not on a cool spring evening. The lane leading to the garden was awash with moonlight and Mike's and my shadows came with us in two crazy out-of-proportion images on the ground.

As we neared the big rocks I felt his hand tighten on mine and he moved off the lane and onto the grass, taking me with him, our shadows disappearing in the circle of darkness surrounding us. We stopped walking and I waited for him to speak and when he didn't, I lifted my face up to find he was looking down at me, his features blurred. I remembered frantically that I didn't really know how to kiss a boy because I had never previously and I knew Mike was going to kiss me and I wanted him to do it.

The doubts, the thoughts, everything evaporated except the enchanting feel of his mouth on mine. A throb which began on my lips flowed all the way through me and the second kiss was even more wonderful and the ones after that, if such a thing was possible. His mouth was soft while his arms circled me like steel bands and both of my arms were around him, although I had no recollection of placing them there.

"Christy . . ." It was a whisper, as faint as the rustle of a breeze.

I drew back a little, ever so little, without actually moving anything except my head. Our bodies curved together and my hands were clasped at the back of his neck, buried in his hair.

"I — uh — guess we'd better go in now,"

he mumbled and his voice had a strangely rough sound.

The unfamiliar feeling inside me must have made me bold. "I'm not sure I want to do that, Mike."

"I know I don't. But it would be smart."

I continued to cling to him and I wanted to stand in that one spot forever with him holding me and kissing me. A new thought seeped into my brain, a frightening thought. If Mike didn't enjoy my kisses as I enjoyed his, if mine didn't satisfy him the way *hers* had done . . . The tormenting fear made me go tense and I was instantly rigid, my hands moving away from Mike's hair to the tweedy cloth on the shoulders of his jacket.

"Christy, listen — " he said in the same rough voice. "We'd better go in. Anyhow, your folks might be looking out of the windows at us and I don't want them to get mad with me. Not tonight, especially. Not ever."

Both of us dropped our arms. I knew what he meant but this was my first experience with a boy and I wondered if the strange sweet current flooding over me was similar to the one in him, making him strong and weak all at the identical moment the way it did me.

It was my idea to walk around the house and come in the front door and I'm not sure why I suggested it. As we crossed the porch with its brightly burning light I glanced at Mike, halfway astonished that he appeared the same as always. I couldn't believe I looked exactly as I had when we left for Sonny's hours before, not when my mouth throbbed from his kisses and my head whirled.

"I'll see you tomorrow night, won't I?" he asked while I was searching in my purse for the house key. We could have rung the bell and summoned one of my parents, but I didn't want to do it.

"I'd like that, Mike."

"If you can get your mother's car tomorrow and want to drive into town, I might be able to grab a little while for a Coke. Between customers, I mean. I couldn't leave the station, but we could sit in your car and at least I'd see you."

The smile I gave him had to be radiant. It couldn't have been less, as happy as I felt.

There was a faint spicy scent in the house and the sound of radio music came from the second floor. To my amazement, nobody was in the den but the room looked especially inviting, the cushions plumped and the newspapers and magazines stacked neatly. The drapes had been drawn with only the lamps left on, not the overhead light.

"Christy, is that you?" My mother came to the top of the stairs.

"Mike's with me," I answered, loving the feel of his name as I spoke.

"The television programs were so dull tonight your daddy and I came upstairs to read and listen to the radio in our room.

If you two are hungry, there's gingerbread in the kitchen."

"So that's what I smell," I murmured. Mike was standing with me and he'd heard everything Mama said. "Are you hungry?" I asked him.

"For gingerbread? Sure. I love the stuff."

The plate of gingerbread, covered with a sheet of clear plastic wrap, was on the counter by the refrigerator and as I poured each of us a glass of milk I reminded myself silently for the second time that evening about how everything really did have a way of working out. I wasn't fooled by my mother's remark about the radio. There was a perfectly good radio on the bookcase in the den. She and Dad often turned it on as they liked to hear music when they were reading. Dad was what Mama termed a "messy reader" as he would toss his newspapers and magazines to the floor when he finished with them, and sometimes after a couple of hours his chair was surrounded by paper. She seldom tidied the den at bedtime, but picked up those papers the following morning when she was straightening the house, only that particular night everything was in place.

I realized Mama and Dad were making it possible for Mike and me to have the den to ourselves and since the family hadn't had gingerbread for dinner and the squares were still warm, she must have baked with us in mind while we were at Sonny's. My mother hadn't forgotten how it was to be a teenager and in her subtle way she was making Mike very welcome.

"Christy, you're smiling," Mike said between bites. "How come?"

"I'm so happy I have to smile. Isn't that reason enough?"

He was standing by the stove, his milk glass in one hand and gingerbread in the other, while I leaned against the sink. Coming to me, he rubbed his cheek gently against mine and agreed that happiness was the best of all reasons to smile.

Chapter

· 13 ·

It was the loveliest spring I could ever remember. Everything was colorful and lush, the leaves popping out on the trees with such suddenness that it was startling to wake up one morning and realize the view of the mountains from the bay window in my room was partially hidden behind a feathery green veil.

Tiny wild violets dotted the yard, their leaves and stems so low to the ground they were barely taller than the grass. Mama discovered hyacinths coming up near the back door and when they bloomed, the flowers were deep blue, as delicately fragrant in their way as the purple lilacs which grew on the tall bushes at the foot of the hill.

My mother was ecstatic at all the growing things. In her garden the lettuce ripened first, maturing early in May with small, crisp green leaves almost sweet in their goodness.

With the end of school looming there was the customary crunch of reports and term papers. Mike, who hated writing anything, groaned at the thought and one Sunday afternoon he brought his notes for a history paper to my house and both of us studied in the backyard. He and I were together every chance we could manage, before classes began, during school lunch periods, and he brought me home in the afternoons. There was no question about our dating on Friday, Saturday, and Sunday nights, but my parents gave a firm veto to my going to the service station to see him.

"The boy has a job, Christy," Dad snapped the Saturday after Mike and I kissed for the first time. The three of us were eating lunch at the kitchen table and I'd asked Mama if I could use her car for a little while. When she said yes and then asked what I planned to do, I made the mistake of saying I was going to meet Mike at the service station for a Coke if he had a lull between customers.

Before I finished the sentence, Dad was shaking his head.

"No, you aren't," he stated flatly. "I know Mike works for his uncle but nobody, and that includes Eben Maxwell, wants an employee goofing off on duty."

"Mike wouldn't be goofing off," I came back defiantly, miffed at my father's straight-laced Victorian outlook. "He'd only talk to me when he didn't have any customers to wait on at the gas pumps."

"*No*, and I mean it, Christy!" My father's tone left little doubt that the subject was closed. I started to tell them my going into town was Mike's idea and that I didn't think he'd have suggested it if he believed his uncle would object, but it seemed best to hush. Later, I wondered if Dad could have been right about Mr. Maxwell as when I told Mike that evening why I hadn't been by to visit him during the afternoon, he shrugged and mumbled that it "probably was just as well."

A couple of weeks later I met Mike's mother. It happened about five-thirty in the afternoon and Mama had asked me to go to the supermarket for a pound of coffee. While I was standing in the checkout line a familiar voice behind me said, "Well, well. Small world, isn't it? Fancy meeting you here."

Twisting around, I was face to face with Mike, who was pushing a grocery cart loaded with food.

"How did you get away from the service station this early?" I asked.

"Mom brought her car in. Something's wrong with the transmission and Uncle Eb told me to drive her home in mine and then said not to bother to come back since it was late. Mom wanted to shop, so here I am." He looked over at a lady who'd been watching us and said, "Mom, this is Christy Jamison."

She was quite small and had Mike's dark hair, although the resemblance stopped at that. Her features were rounder than his, her hands and feet tiny, and I marveled that she could be the mother of a six-footer.

"Your father manages the motor plant, doesn't he?" she said to me. "He must be a big improvement over the last manager from what everyone says. What was that other man's name, Mike? Garlow?"

"Harlow," Mike and I replied in unison.

The checker was ready for me and I laid my pound can of coffee on the counter. "See you later, Christy," Mike said. I told Mrs. Maxwell I was happy to have met her, and she smiled at me in such an impersonal way I had the feeling she didn't know that Mike and I were dating. Boys' families probably never knew the way a girl's family did, I decided. When a boy left his house he didn't have to announce what he was going to do and with whom, not the way girls did. Correction: not the way *I* did.

At the end of April my parents relented about my seeing Mike on school nights. I'd been begging them, and they finally gave in, with the stipulation that he could come to the house one evening during the week for an hour, Mama cautioning me that if I didn't send him home when the time was up, either she or Dad would do it. Mike chose Wednesdays, and on other evenings he'd phone. My mother usually signaled me to ring off after thirty minutes as she seemed to think that was long enough for us to talk, and I knew we'd never have enough time for all the things to be said. There were kisses, of course — warm, tantalizing kisses when we were alone.

"I'm not crazy about your folks' strictness where you're concerned," Mike commented one day with a grin. "But I have to admit I'm keeping up with school stuff better than I used to. You must be having a good influence on me, Christy. Maybe I'll make some decent grades for a change."

Than I used to could be interpreted to mean, "When I was dating Jill." From little hints Betsy had dropped, I'd learned that Jill Rogers dated almost every night and wasn't concerned if her report card was loaded with D's and F's. I was surprised that Mike had managed to pass during the time he went steady with her and I knew he'd had warnings from several teachers because of the drop in his grades. The "than I used to" was as close as Mike had come to mentioning Jill to me, which suited me because I didn't want to talk or think about her. We'd seen her a few times when we stopped at Sonny's and she was always with Vince Halloran, and while occasionally they paused to say hello or chat briefly, they hadn't lingered.

On weekends Mike and I stayed at my house, sitting in the yard if the weather was good, or we went to the movies or teamed up with Betsy and Gordon. Bud often tagged along, sometimes dating Sharon Park, a senior, a girl I thought was rather mousy looking with the personality to match, although I didn't say that aloud. After I got to know her I liked her and it was interesting to discover there was at least one girl in the world who was more shy than I was — or than I'd *been*. Betsy, who had succeeded in persuading Bud to call Sharon for a date, confided to me she was sure they'd be perfect together.

"Why do you think so?" I asked. "She's awfully quiet."

"Bud's a sweet guy but he doesn't assert himself, and he'll have to take some initiative with Sharon unless they want to spend an entire date in silence. This ought to give him the self-confidence he needs."

"Or scare him to death where girls are concerned. Do you think Sharon can get his mind off of Jill?"

"Who knows?" Betsy sighed. "I honestly doubt if anybody can do that. If Jill and Vince split, Bud will be right there at Jill's feet like an obedient puppy dog. I can't believe any fellow as smart in school as Bud is, when he wants to study, can't see through Jill, and she's practically rude to him unless she wants something. He soaks it up like a wet dishrag. That's Bud, though. He never stands up to anybody."

One Friday in the middle of May Mike asked if I objected to his bringing Bud when he came over that night, and of course I said it was fine but to be honest, I'd rather have had Mike to myself. It never ceased to amaze me how protective the others were about Bud, as if they knew his physical ugliness was a thing he had to endure. Bud, Mike, and I played Monopoly that night and after a while rode out to a drive-in for milk shakes.

The next evening, Mike and I were sitting on the big rocks in the backyard when I made the mistake of telling him about an incident which happened earlier in the day. It was one of those long, lazy spring nights when the daylight lingered with a pearly glow in the sky and even though it was after eight, full darkness hadn't come.

"Guess who phoned me this afternoon?" I said.

"Who?" he asked casually.

Without giving a name, I said it was a boy, my voice with a teasing tone although Mike didn't take it in a jolly fashion. His mouth hardened and he twisted around so he was facing me.

"What boy, Christy?" he demanded harshly. "Don't tell me it was Bud! I'll wring his neck if it was!"

"Vince Halloran phoned."

"Vince called you, Christy? What the hell for?" He sounded furious.

I wished desperately I hadn't mentioned Vince's call. At the time it happened it struck me as funny and yet, I'd been flattered. Now, I didn't want to talk about it but apparently Mike wasn't going to let the matter die as he jumped up from the rock and stood in front of me, his feet wide apart and his hands on his hips.

"I-I think he — he wanted me to go out with him," I stammered.

"Doesn't he know you're dating me? What did you tell him?"

"That I already had plans for the weekend."

Mike's shoulders drooped ever so slightly as if he was relaxing but he continued to scowl. "Of all the brazen guts! That joker ought to have his jaw busted for trying to crash in! He thinks he's God's gift to females!"

"There's no reason for you to get excited over it, Mike. I'm sorry I said anything to you about it."

"Vince would use you, Christy!" He made a fist out of his right hand and banged it into his left palm. "He and Jill must have had a fight and he probably was looking around for a way to make her jealous."

Isn't that what you did once? I thought it but didn't utter it, chilled to my bones in the balmy air with the memory.

I knew Mike liked me now, but sometimes I couldn't help wondering if I had actually replaced Jill Rogers in his life. He might not want to be with her every day any longer, although I didn't doubt he wanted some of the things she'd given him. Lots of laughs and fun. Sex? I didn't know and didn't dare consider the possibility.

If only Mike would say, "Doesn't Vince Halloran know you're my girl, Christy?" I'd shed my concern, but as it was, the doubts lingered and pulled at me the way a stubborn hangnail makes you conscious of a sore fingertip. Until Mike called me his girl, until he said it aloud, I knew I couldn't feel secure about us and our relationship. Betsy had said if Jill and Vince broke up Bud would be at her feet like an obedient puppy dog, and I didn't let myself consider the awful possibility that Mike, also, might go running at her beck and call.

Chapter

· 14 ·

Summer swooped down on us early in June
with such a blast of unseasonable heat that
the final days of school were miserable. The
last exam period fell on a Thursday morning
and at noon that day Mike and I met Betsy,
Gordon, Sharon, and Bud at Sonny's for
lunch, discovering plenty of other students
were ahead of us with the same idea and we
had to wait for a table. We stood just under
the arch leading to the back room so we could
watch in both directions and grab the first
empty seats.

"Man, I'm ready for a vacation from
everything connected with school and I mean
everything," Gordon announced when we
were in a booth. "Why don't we celebrate tonight? No more homework for three whole
months! Wow!"

Betsy suggested going to Coburn's Lake for a swim and taking supper with us. The lake was some twenty miles away and I'd heard enough about it to know it was privately owned and that Mr. Coburn charged admission, stopping the swimming at 7 P.M., although he kept the picnic grounds open until nine.

"Do you have to work the usual hours today?" I asked Mike.

"I can probably get off early. Uncle Eb's good about letting me leave for special outings if I don't ask too often."

"I have to practice for graduation," Sharon said in her low voice.

The diploma ceremony was scheduled for the following night and I suppose the rest of us overlooked it since we were winding up our junior years while Sharon had been a senior.

"Go on and tell them your plans, Sharon," Bud nodded to her.

She was leaving the first of the week for Richmond to enroll in a business college for a secretarial course, she said. All of us knew she'd been thinking about going there in September although the change in date was a surprise.

"The school notified me day before yesterday that there are some openings for the term starting in a few days and my family thinks I'd only be killing time if I sat out the summer here," she added.

Glancing at Bud, I hoped he would miss

her enough to keep in touch with her. Their dating seemed almost as impersonal as if she'd been his cousin. Nothing in his face gave an indication of what he was thinking and he concentrated on tearing the crusts off his chicken salad sandwich, taking pains not to leave a speck of meat or mayonnaise on the part of the bread he discarded.

I knew a little about the others' summer plans. Gordon and Bud would begin work Monday at the ice cream plant on the edge of town with the same jobs they'd had the previous summer. Mike had told me Vince Halloran was already working there.

Betsy moaned off and on during the spring about having to go to Maryland to spend six weeks with her grandmother when school ended.

"I love Granny but it's awfully boring there," she commented earlier.

"Will you be in Greenview all summer, Christy?" Gordon asked me.

"Most of it," I answered. "We usually spend the last two weeks of July in Indiana visiting relatives."

"I want to go to the beach," Mike said. "Think your folks would let you come with me, Christy? We could leave on a Friday and come back Sunday night."

I knew they wouldn't, not if it was only Mike and me on an overnight trip, but I kept quiet and I don't think the others noticed as they were making plans for the outing to Coburn's Lake. Mike must have known the answer before he asked the question as he didn't say any more about it.

That evening was the start and the finish of lots of things.

Bud was alone again, and Betsy and Gordon seemed very conscious that their time together would end temporarily in a few days when she went to Maryland. As for Mike and me, in an indirect way we settled something important which I guess had been on both of our minds although we'd never talked about it. That came later, after we left the lake and were in my yard.

Since the boys were paying the admission fees, Betsy and I offered to provide the supper. Mama helped me, stirring up a batch of cupcakes while I deviled eggs and made pimento and cheese sandwiches. Betsy was to bring potato salad and cold cuts, and my mother must have reminded me a dozen times to keep everything in the ice chest until we were ready to eat or we'd be sure to have food poisoning in such hot weather.

The lake shimmered under a bright blue sky. There was a narrow white beach — Gordon said the sand had to be brought in on trucks every year — and on the far bank the woods were as thick as a jungle. Stooping down, I trailed my hand in the water and shivered. Mike explained that even though the air was warm, the lake was fed by underground springs and it took many days of hot sunshine to change the water temperature, adding with a wink that if I got really chilled he'd put his arms around me and heat me up in a hurry.

When you think you know someone well and then see him or her in swim trunks or a bathing suit, it can be a shock. I was glad to be naturally slim although seeing Betsy's curves made me aware that I had very few and it was hard not to envy her on that score as she filled her red bikini more attractively than I did my one-piece yellow suit. We came out of the dressing room to find the boys were already in the water, Mike swimming toward a float anchored some thirty feet from shore. He cut through the water with long, clean strokes and when he reached the float and swung himself up on it in one quick action, the muscles in his back and chest gleamed under the wet skin. Mike's body was beautiful, with broad shoulders and a flat waist and hips. Gordon was almost scrawny without his shirt and Bud's body build seemed to accent his odd-shaped head. Mike saw me and waved and I swam out to join him, hoping I looked graceful and that I glided across the lake as effortlessly as he did, knowing I didn't.

We were in and out of the lake until the whistle blew at seven and then we moved to one of the tables in the picnic area, sitting on wooden benches so splintery we had to spread our damp bath towels across them to protect our legs. Only a few other people were around, all of them far enough away for us to have one corner to ourselves.

Everything was serene, the sun going

lower in the western sky until it was completely out of sight and the air becoming cooler while lake water made a soft lapping sound against the sand. I leaned against Mike's shoulder, feeling the sturdy strength of his body as his arm went around me. A little water clung to his hair and if he moved his head there was a damp shower on my arm. Once I turned toward him and felt his mouth brush my temple.

Across the table from us, Gordon's arm was around Betsy. Bud sat alone at the end of the table. He'd ripped open the potato chip bag and was picking up the last broken bits, licking his forefinger and sliding it over the crumbs, every few seconds plunging the end of that finger into his mouth. I wondered if he missed Sharon, or if he was thinking about Jill. Playing with the potato chip crumbs must have been simply something to do as he couldn't possibly have needed food, not as much as he'd eaten.

Bud, who'd brought Gordon and Betsy, drove them home at nine when the lake grounds closed. Mike and I didn't talk much on the way to Greenview and he steered the car with one hand, the other arm around me. I was so tired from having taken a hard exam that morning, rushing to get my share of the picnic prepared, and the exertion of the first swim of the season that I could have gone to sleep, but wouldn't let myself do it.

At the house there was a note on the kitchen table from Mama saying she and Dad were playing bridge with friends and would be home around eleven.

"Christy, let's go outside," Mike said and we walked down to the big rocks.

The night air was filled with the soft fragrance of flowers. There was no moon but the stars glistened and glimmered over us and the leaves fluttered noiselessly on the trees. I was eager for Mike to put his arms around me but I wasn't prepared for the wildness of those kisses. His mouth touched mine and something exploded in both of us. I felt myself being pulled tightly against his strangely unfamiliar body, aching for that kiss to go on and on and knowing desperately it must stop.

A sob caught in my chest, strangling me. With massive effort I managed to get my palms flat against him and twist free.

"Christy, don't," he begged hoarsely and reached for me again.

I backed away, stepping out of the circle of his arms. "I can't, Mike."

"Can't what? You're not making sense."

I swallowed and in spite of it, the lump in my throat grew and grew so that I was unable to speak at first. My heartbeats sounded like a tom-tom and a roaring noise filled my ears.

"I-I guess I'm just not ready yet for — for more than kissing."

"But you're human! You're bound to want me the same as I want you. If you really care about me — "

The sentence hung between us, unfinished. In the silence I heard the lonely wail of a whippoorwill and when I looked at the sky because I had to look at something and didn't trust myself to gaze at Mike, the stars were peeping through the leaves on the tree branches just as they always had. Somehow I'd expected the whole universe to be different.

"I shouldn't have spoken to you like I just did," Mike sighed.

Suddenly my knees gave way and I sat down on the stone bench. He started to pace in front of me, going ten or twelve feet and jerking around to cover the distance again. I knew what he wanted and I knew Jill probably would have agreed if she'd been there instead of me. Maybe he wished she was there.

"Please don't hate me," I pleaded. "If I led you on I didn't mean to do it and I'm sorry about — about everything. I'm sorry if I'm not the kind of girl you want. But I can't help it. I really do care for you, Mike, care more than I've ever cared for a boy. Maybe more than I could ever care for anyone else. I want you to kiss me and I love having your arms around me, but . . . not more than that."

He stopped his pacing and stooped down, his chin level with my knees. I wanted to reach out and touch him, but I didn't. Tears were tangled in my lashes, making it hard for me to see him, even though his face was so near mine I could feel the fluttery warmth of his breath.

"You quit worrying." He managed a one-sided smile. "I couldn't hate you if I tried to do it, Christy Jamison. Don't you know that?"

I hoped it was true, hoped with all my heart.

"Come to think of it," he went on as he straightened up and took a seat beside me, slipping one arm around my shoulders, "I guess I ought to award you a medal or something. You sure make it easy for me to behave myself and that's a compliment whether it sounds like one or not. Right now I don't want to stop kissing you or stop anything else, but in the morning I'll be glad you have enough willpower for both of us."

Chapter

·15·

The long summer hours melted together like pats of butter on a warm dish, each day so similar to the one before I could scarcely keep them separate in my mind. With Betsy and Sharon out of town and Mike at work, I expected to be lonely, maybe even a tiny bit bored until evening, and it wasn't that way at all.

I missed seeing Mike during the daytime but giving up the school grind was a relief and it was nice to be able to read what I wanted instead of text books and references. I did my share of the household chores as well as helped Mother in the garden, and after a time I realized there was a bonus in those activities as my mother and I were recapturing the intimacy we'd shared during the first days in Greenview when we didn't know anyone but each other. We'd grown apart when I began dating Mike and now, in late June, we came full circle again.

I couldn't tell Mama everything. I couldn't mention the sweetness of Mike's kisses or how my heart quickened at his touch, but she and I talked and laughed together once more and I decided some of the comfortable feeling between us had developed because we were no longer totally dependent on one another for companionship. She now had friends and things to do, and I had the precious moments with Mike.

Dad seemed more relaxed, too. Things were going well at the motor plant and the production schedule was up. Mama told me he'd had letters of praise from company officials, adding almost smugly, "I knew Bryan was the man for the job here. He thrives on a challenge."

As June came to an end, the flower section of the garden was a mass of blooms, the tall spikes of blue delphinium making a backdrop for pink phlox and white begonias. Blackeyed Susans, their yellow petals pulled back to expose the velvety brown centers, alternated with clumps of white shasta daisies, and a border of scarlet geraniums seemed to be vying with red and purple petunias to see which would be more colorful. Marigolds and asters would come later and so would the pert blue bachelor's buttons, as those plants were covered with buds. We had flowers in every room in the house and I loved cutting the blossoms and arranging them in vases.

Each day Mama and I weeded and picked vegetables. The early corn was tender and juicy, and there was gooseneck squash which went well with tiny pearl onions. The thick leaves of curly kale were Dad's favorite although I didn't care much for that, and I could scarcely wait for the tomatoes to ripen. Green peppers and beets were "coming along," as Mama phrased it, and we had to make a string trellis so the beans could climb, snap beans in one spot and tiny butter beans in another.

"Are you planning to open a boarding-house, Susan?" Dad asked Mama one afternoon when he came in from work to find a bushel basket of freshly picked peas on the back steps, another bushel in the kitchen and me at the table, shelling peas as hard as I could. Mama was making dinner which included a saucepan of peas simmering on the stove.

"I raised a larger crop than I expected," she laughed. "Don't worry. They won't be wasted. I'm freezing what we can't eat now — and I'll warn you that you'll be exposed to plenty of them in the immediate future."

After dinner Mama and I returned to the shelling with Dad pitching in to help, and we were still doing it when Mike arrived. He asked if we needed another worker and Dad said quickly, "The more the merrier."

Mike drew a chair up beside me and went

to work, dropping what he shelled into the yellow mixing bowl where I was putting mine, tossing the empty pods into a brown paper bag on the floor. As we finished that bushel and began on another Dad started to hum, a habit he had when he was doing something which involved using his hands but not his mind. He had a baritone voice and Mama joined in with the words to the song. So did Mike and I, one tune following another from the latest popular hits to country music. As one melody ended, a new one was begun and all of us participated, humming or whistling if we didn't remember the words.

"I actually believe we've finished shelling," Mama said when the final bushel was done.

"You mean you're not going to run to the garden and pick another batch by moonlight?" Dad teased.

"I won't dignify that remark with an answer." Turning from Dad to Mike, she said, "I'm going to send some peas home with you, Mike. Shelled but not cooked, and I want you to put them in your car right now or you might forget them later."

"Please don't forget, Mike." Dad pretended to groan. "If you leave them here I'll have to eat them. Probably scrambled with my eggs for breakfast."

"That's another remark I won't dignify with an answer," Mama came back. "You may not get any breakfast at all if you say much more."

"Mom will be glad to get the peas but I'll

feel like a cannibal seeing those cute little green things on my plate," Mike said. "In the last hour I think I've developed a sort of personal relationship with them. Mrs. Jamison, did you really mean to have so many or was it an accident?"

That broke Dad up. He laughed so hard his face turned red, and Mama and I joined in.

Some boys wouldn't have been satisfied to sit in the kitchen with a girl's parents and they'd have resented doing something like shelling peas, never volunteering to help as Mike had done. Maybe those other guys would have considered it unmanly. I knew positively there wasn't anything unmanly about Mike Maxwell, and as he carried a quart jar of shelled peas to his automobile I felt very glad he was the way he was. Glad, too, that he fitted in so beautifully with my family.

Chapter

· 16 ·

If things are going smoothly it's hard to believe small incidents can be devastating. The first of July I was lulled into thinking the remainder of the summer would be as pleasant as the start had been, and it didn't take long for me to discover my mistake. Nothing about the month developed as I anticipated.

With July came the summer heat, although the nights were delightful, cool enough for a thin cotton blanket to feel just right across my body when I was in bed. We'd brought our three air conditioners with us when we moved to Greenview and while occasionally one of them was turned on during the middle of the day, it seldom was needed for long at a time, and never after dark. Being in the mountains kept us from the scorching summer temperatures I'd known in the past and when I said that to Mike, it made him smile. He loved the Blue Ridge and vowed he could imagine nothing more drab than living in a flat area where it was miserably sticky and hot for weeks on end.

The first day of July I asked Mike what sort of celebration Greenview would have on the Fourth. "You've got to be kidding, Christy," he came back.

We were sitting on the rock bench in my yard, watching the final traces of twilight fade. Invisible insects made a soft buzz in the grass and the lightning bugs were out, their tiny bodies glowing vivid yellow as they moved lazily from one spot to another.

"You mean this town doesn't do anything to celebrate?" I persisted. "Not even a band concert or fireworks? The other places I've lived always had fireworks."

"We used to have them. The Fire Department did a firework show for a while. But then they stopped."

A leaf blew into my lap. Picking it up, I held it on my fingertips and let it float to the ground. "It's still a big holiday, Mike. What do people here do now?"

"Mostly they go out of town. A lot of them take a weekend or a week's vacation the first of July. I only get one day off for the Fourth but we can do something if you want."

I did want. Mike and I had been to Coburn's Lake so often to swim it didn't seem special enough for a holiday. "What about the State Park?" I asked. It was seventy-five miles away.

"The park is always so crowded on holidays, Christy. Why don't we go to Coburn's this time and try the State Park later in the month?"

"Coburn's is all right" — I drew a long breath — "but later in the month I'll be in Indiana." My mouth felt dry when I said it and instantly I realized I didn't want to go to the Midwest. The thought of having miles between Mike and me was gruesome.

He asked questions about the trip and I explained that every summer for as far back as I could remember, Mama and I had flown to Indiana in July to visit relatives. A week later Dad joined us, driving out, and at the end of the second week the three of us returned together in the car.

Over two weeks without seeing Mike . . . without kissing him or talking to him or watching him smile. . . . It seemed as long as an eternity and thinking about it made me ache. "I'll miss you," I said, and leaned against him.

"Do you have to go, Christy? Couldn't you beg off?"

"You know Mama and Dad would never let me stay here alone."

He spread his long legs straight out, digging his heels into the earth, the toes of his sneakers pointed up. "What about going for only one week, not two?" he asked. "Your mother could stay in Indiana two weeks if she wants, and you could stay here to keep house for your dad and tend to the garden. When your dad goes, you'd ride out with him, and you and I wouldn't be apart but a little over a week."

If I only could! The joyous hope swirled inside of me like a spinning top and I told Mike I'd talk to Mama first thing in the morning.

About nine o'clock that night Mike and I rode into town to Sonny's, which was practically deserted. The back room was dark and just a few people were in the front area with everything strangely subdued since the jukebox was silent. Three old-fashioned ceiling fans rotated slowly overhead, not making it cooler, but circulating the air. We took a booth and decided on strawberry ice cream cones, Mike going to the soda fountain for them and returning with a fistful of paper napkins to catch the drips. Already little pink streams were trickling down the sides of both cones to his fingers.

Before we finished eating, Gordon came in and joined us in the booth. I'd seen very little of him since school closed and Betsy left for her grandmother's, and I thought he looked tired. He yawned twice and the second time gave a sheepish grin with the comment that getting up in time to be at work at six A.M. at the ice cream plant had just about convinced him he ought to go to bed earlier at night.

"Christy and I are trying to create some action for the Fourth," Mike said. "Want to come with us to Coburn's or the State Park?"

"Coburn's," I cut in and saw Mike smile. If he preferred Coburn's, it was all right with me.

"I'm going to see Betsy over the Fourth," Gordon replied. "Have you talked to Bud lately? He and Sharon might want to do something, Mike."

Mike said he hadn't seen Bud in the last few days.

"Sharon's school has a three-day break for the holiday and she'll be in town," Gordon went on. Picking up the only unused paper napkin on the table, he began twisting the corner into a string, rolling it between his thumb and forefinger until it coiled like a pig's tail. "Know something?" he said. "I believe Bud's actually getting to really like that girl."

Mike's comment was, "Bud could do worse," and Gordon gave a yep. They were so careful not to talk about Sharon I wondered what they would have said if they'd been by themselves. There was an unwritten rule on that sort of conversation. Boys didn't talk about girls in front of girls any more than girls — smart girls, that is — discussed one boy in the hearing of another.

Getting to his feet and yawning again, Gordon muttered, "Guess I'll be shoving off," and started away, sticking his hands into the back pockets of his jeans. He took three or four steps and turned toward us once more. "Were you surprised about Vince, Mike?" he asked.

Mike and I were alert instantly. "What about Vince?" Mike said.

"You didn't know Vince had left town?"

I guess my astonishment showed in my face the way Mike's did in his. A couple of weeks earlier we'd bumped into Vince and Jill as we were coming out of the movies and exchanged hellos without really talking as they were on their way in. I hadn't seen either of them since that night and if Mike had, he'd failed to say anything about it.

Gordon came back to the booth but didn't sit down. "Apparently Vince pulled out Sunday night," he said. "When he didn't show up for work Monday, everybody including Jim Carpenter, the foreman, thought he was sick but he didn't call in or come in Tuesday, either. Carpenter tried to get in touch with him and couldn't, but Vince's mother was at the house and said his bed hadn't been slept in when she woke up Monday. Vince's car was gone and he'd taken all his clothes and some other stuff. His portable TV and fishing tackle box and — get this! His skis and that heavy red jacket lined with sheepskin he wears in real cold weather. If he took his winter duds in the middle of the summer, that sounds to me as if he's gone for a long time."

"Where did he go?" Mike asked.

Gordon shrugged. "Who knows?"

"Didn't he leave a message?" I said.

"Didn't he leave his mother a note? Hasn't she tried to find him or notify the police?"

"He's not a kid, Christy. Vince is nineteen, practically twenty, and nobody can make him hang around Greenview if he doesn't want to live here. The cops wouldn't step in unless he'd committed a crime or they thought he'd been kidnapped or forced to go against his will."

Gordon picked up the twisted paper napkin and began playing with it again. "I don't suppose his mother cares much one way or the other," he went on. "She's strange. Real hard to get along with. Mr. Halloran left years ago and I guess Vince got tired of having her boss him. Carpenter said she seemed to think Vince might be in Ohio where he was working when he went off after he quit school. His married sister lives in Ohio."

The three overhead fans droned faintly. A group of men standing at the soda fountain talking to Sonny burst into harsh laughter and the three of us glanced in that direction, jarred by the unexpected sound. I heard Mike clear his throat and say, "Where does Jill think Vince is?"

That identical question had been burning my tongue and I'd tried to ask it, unable to put it into words. Jill would know Vince Halloran's whereabouts if anyone did, as they'd been inseparable since he came back to Greenview in the winter, but I couldn't bring myself to mention her. It was impossible for me to forget she'd been Mike's girl.

"Jill's at Virginia Beach," Gordon said.

"Went down last week with her brother and sister-in-law and they're paying her expenses so she can babysit their kids. I think they're supposed to come home tonight or tomorrow. If Vince didn't tell Jill his plans, she'll have some homecoming and . . . hey — "

He hushed, staring first at Mike and then at me, his eyebrows lifting. "What gives with you two?" he barked. "Do you hibernate? I never see you anymore and you've sure been out of circulation if you didn't know Jill was away or that Vince had left town or about Sharon coming home for three days."

His tone was almost an accusation, and while there was no reason for me to feel ashamed, I had a hot, uncomfortable sensation. It hadn't occurred to me that Mike and I stayed to ourselves most of the time, but Gordon's words made me realize we did, and to be truthful, that suited me. Mike seemed content at my house even when we watched TV in the den with Mama and Dad, or if he helped with some everyday chore like shelling peas, and I knew he enjoyed the times we were in the backyard alone, enjoyed them as much as I did. With the big rocks to shield us from the house, our stone bench was private. We could lose ourselves in the tender kisses.

"Maybe Jill and Vince have broken up," Mike commented, ignoring Gordon's pointed question about us. There was a growl in Mike's tone which made me wonder what he was thinking. "Maybe that's the reason Vince left. One reason, anyhow."

"Vince might be at Virginia Beach with Jill right now." Gordon had the entire paper napkin in a string and he curled it around his thumb, then dropped it on the table. "This time I really am going." He grinned and headed for the door.

Something about the set to Mike's jaws let me know the peaceful feeling from earlier in the evening had vanished. While I was looking at him, frown lines appeared in his forehead and the small pulse in his left temple throbbed hard, the way it always did when he was using a lot of self-control. It could have been a delayed reaction to Gordon's crack about our hibernating, but I saw no reason for Mike to be really mad and he was getting angry fast.

I waited for him to speak, and when he didn't, I said, "Remember me? I'm the girl you brought to Sonny's tonight and I'm still here."

"Christy, did you know about Vince's leaving town?"

"Me?" The word came out as a gasp. "Why would I know? If I had, don't you think I'd have said something about it? What do you mean?"

"Why not you?" Mike's lips thinned out. "Vince wanted to date you a while back so why wouldn't he try to do it again, especially if Jill was away?"

It was hard to believe what I was hearing and I couldn't have been any more stunned if I'd been doused with ice water. The way Mike stared at me hurt, his eyes flinty and his mouth tight, and I opened my lips to storm at him that it wasn't fun to be blamed for what didn't happen and that even if Vince had been in touch with me — which he hadn't — it wouldn't have been a mortal sin.

But before I could say anything like that, the tortured expression on Mike's face made me realize he was suffering. Instead of giving a snippy answer to his ugly question about Vince, I leaned across the table and covered both of his hands with mine, the first time I'd ever touched him like that in a public place.

"Why should I care what Vince does, Mike?" I asked. "I haven't seen him or talked to him since the other evening when we passed him with Jill at the movies, and if you want the truth, I don't believe I've given him a thought from then until now."

He flushed, his hands gripping mine as the frown lines eased out of his forehead. "Sorry I came on so strong," he muttered. "Let's knock off talking about Vince. Oh, Christy! Why am I forever apologizing to you? I never had to do that to other girls I've dated!"

I didn't know how to reply. I hadn't asked for an apology and certainly didn't want to cause Mike unhappiness, but I couldn't deny feeling an exciting surge flowing through my body, coming from the new knowledge that I could arouse all sorts of emotions in him. I'd never felt it before and it made my blood race.

But before my satisfaction turned to smugness another thought shot into my mind, the frightening realization that once again Mike had failed to let me know he considered me his girl. He hadn't said, "Why would Vince try to date *my girl*?" and he'd lumped me right with the unnamed mass he designated as "other girls I've dated."

He might feel he was apologizing, but I'd been the one who kept us out of a major argument. I'd reached out to touch his hands. It hadn't been the other way around. Gazing down at the marble-topped table in the booth, I studied the dark veins and myriads of scratches on the milky surface, wondering if a girl ever felt truly sure of a boy, or if something was wrong with me because I continued to have the dreadful fear that eventually I'd lose Mike to *her*.

Her meant just one person in the world. Apparently Jill Rogers had only to smile a certain way and the boys would begin running to her side, not just Bud and Vince, but Mike, too.

Chapter
·17·

The Fourth of July was a terrible day. Not the weather which was hot and dry the way the Fourth traditionally is supposed to be, but because everything was wrong from the time I came downstairs that morning until Mike told me good night.

Mama and I had an argument while I was helping her prepare breakfast, and it was my fault since I made the error of mentioning the Indiana trip again. She and I were eating alone as Dad was playing golf. At noon she was going to meet him for lunch at the golf club.

During the previous two days I'd begged to be allowed to stay in Virginia with Dad until he drove to Indiana and my mother acted as if I were asking for a keg of diamonds. The idea was ridiculous, she stated firmly every time I brought up the trip. She even refused to change her mind after I asked Dad and he gave an iffy answer by remarking, "Well, it's all right with me, I suppose, if your mother approves."

"I do not approve," Mama said. "And I'm tired of discussing it."

When I asked her why I couldn't stay, she had a dozen reasons. Among other things Dad would have me on his mind, she said. She didn't like to think of my running all over town alone or being in the house alone for seven days, and Aunt Doris would be hurt if I didn't care enough about my relatives to spend two weeks with them.

On the Fourth I should have known better than to try to discuss anything before breakfast, but the separation from Mike was uppermost in my thoughts and every day brought it nearer. Mama had already informed me we weren't waiting until the last two weeks in the month to leave for the Midwest, as it was more convenient this year for Aunt Doris to have us there earlier and we'd be flying to Indiana on the tenth, which was less than a week away.

"Christy, please don't start in again about your not going to Indiana when I go," Mama said snappishly on the morning of the Fourth, and she flipped the bacon over too quickly in the skillet. Hot grease splattered out on the stove. "You are going when I go and that's final."

"Aren't you forgetting I'm sixteen now, Mama? It seems to me I ought to be able to make a few decisions for myself, but you treat me as though I were in kindergarten."

The look she tossed in my direction would have melted steel and I wished I'd kept quiet. Letting the subject go, I decided silently to try once more when she was in a better mood.

I carried our orange juice over to the table by the bay window and Mama followed with the bacon and toast. "What time are you and Mike going to Coburn's Lake?" she asked.

"Whenever he wants. The middle of the afternoon, I guess."

Her eyebrows went up and I thought she was annoyed at the idea of having to help me pack a lunch. "Don't worry about a picnic," I said quickly. "It probably will be so crowded at the lake we can't get a table, so we'll just swim and buy some hamburgers on the way back tonight."

"Christy, I really don't want you on the highway tonight. This is one of the most dangerous times of year for accidents, especially after dark, and I'd rather you and Mike came on home while it's daylight."

"Oh, Mama." I gave an exasperated groan. "There you go, treating me like a child again! Our plans are made."

"It would be very easy to change them."

"No, it wouldn't," I said in a belligerent tone. "It's not just us, Mike and me, but Bud and Sharon are coming, too." I almost added that their parents hadn't objected to their being on the road after dark, but didn't say it. For one reason, I didn't actually know how the Warrens or the Parks felt about any-thing, and for another, I'd learned a long time before that few statements angered my mother more quickly than for me to try to sway her by claiming, "Everybody else does it."

"After all, Mama, just because it's a holi-day doesn't mean we'll be in danger," I rattled on. "I guess I could have a fatal accident any old time, coming out of our drive in broad daylight. Just because Mike and I'll be driving back from the lake on the night of the Fourth of July won't automati-cally make us statistics. He's a very good driver."

"Please don't say any more about highway statistics. Mike may be the most careful driver in the world, but it's the other driver I'm thinking about. You never know what that other driver will do." She took a long sip of coffee. "I suppose it's all right for you and your friends to go, but . . . Well, please don't be late."

She should have known we wouldn't be late. I commented on how blue the mountains looked in the morning sunlight and we fin-ished the meal without more fiery words. She went upstairs to make the beds while I did the breakfast dishes.

Mike arrived shortly after eleven with several cans of soda packed in an ice chest in the back of his car, and his swim trunks wrapped in a blue towel on the front seat. We'd planned in advance to eat lunch at my house and since it was too early for that, I got out a jigsaw puzzle and we spread the pieces on the kitchen table.

A pleasant breeze came through the door and the tree branches filtered the sunlight, sparing us the warmth as well as the glare. A little later Mama poked her head in the kitchen to say good-bye and Mike gave a low whistle, grinning at her. She looked attractive in a new ecru linen dress trimmed with braid just a tiny shade deeper tan on the sleeves and around the square neckline, and her skin was a golden color from so many hours of working in the garden.

"I hope that whistle was a compliment, Mike," she said and smiled at him.

"It sure was. You ought to model for a fashion magazine, Mrs. Jamison."

"I doubt that, but thanks anyway. You children be careful on the road."

"Children." Mike's eyes met mine and we laughed as Mama went out. "Do parents always think of their kids as 'children'?"

"Mine do." I sighed. "Mama still won't give in about my coming to Indiana with Dad." I didn't want to spoil the day talking about it, and to get my thoughts away from the frustration of having to do what my parents wanted instead of what I'd have preferred I asked Mike what time we picked up Bud and Sharon.

"We don't pick them up," he answered. "They're coming here to get us and we'll go with them. I dropped a hint to Bud that it was his turn to drive because I've furnished the gas plenty lately. They're coming around two o'clock." Mike fitted a border piece into the puzzle and added, "Have you seen Sharon since she came home?"

I hadn't. "Yesterday I phoned her just to gab but there wasn't any answer at her house. Bud's happy about her being here, isn't he?"

"I guess he is. He stopped at the station yesterday but I was too busy to spend much time with him. The day before a holiday everybody in town wants gas."

We had ham sandwiches and slices of ripe, red tomatoes from the garden for our lunch, eating while we finished the jigsaw, and I was sliding the final piece into place when Bud's car came up the hill. Both of us heard it and without pausing, I began taking the puzzle apart, dropping the pieces into the box. Mike caught his breath and muttered, "Of all the . . . ," without ending the sentence which made me look out of the back door.

Bud had swerved the car so the passenger side was toward the house, and the girl with him saw Mike and me watching and she waved, the sunshine picking up the highlights of her dazzling auburn hair. He'd brought Jill instead of Sharon Park.

There was a strange stiffness in my body the entire afternoon. Everything was too much, the colors too intense, the reflection of the sun on the lake too white and shiny, the odor of French fries and greasy hot dogs coming from the concession stand mingling with the smell of onions and suntan lotion.

Coburn's Lake was so crowded we couldn't get into the regular parking area and had to leave the car a quarter of a mile down the road, trudging on the scorching pavement which must have been melting the soles of our sneakers since I smelled the putrid odor of burning rubber.

Jill talked constantly in her bubbling way on the drive to the lake. She and Bud were in front and she sat sideways with her back in the corner, one shoulder against the car window, so she could look at Mike and me in the rear. Mike talked a little and Bud talked a lot, laughing too loud at just about every remark Jill made. I said practically nothing.

"Oh, brother." Mike groaned in an apprehensive way after we paid our admission fee and went past the fence and shrubbery which hid the lake from the road. I knew how he felt. People were wall-to-wall, the lake jammed, and most of the sandy strip was covered with beach towels. Little kids roamed everywhere, splashing water and throwing balls and stepping on the feet of sunbathers. Globs of food and watermelon rinds which hadn't been put into trash cans had attracted flies, and when we finally located a vacant spot for the four of us, I had to scuff dirt over what was left of a chocolate-covered doughnut which someone had dropped and which now was swarming with ants. We were under the trees and well away from the water, but it was the only place available.

The bath house was a nightmare. Jill and I couldn't get a booth or a locker so we put on our swim suits in the open space in the center of the dressing area with an audience of women of all ages. I didn't consider myself overly modest, and in the gym at school there was no privacy in the girls' locker room, but this was as public as outside. We changed quickly and when we rejoined the fellows we had to carry our clothes with us as we knew they'd be stolen if we left them on a bench in the building. The only good angle from my point of view was that Jill and I didn't have to talk to each other amid the commotion around us.

Jill was everywhere at once, running from group to group, speaking to people she knew, flirting openly with every guy who responded to her smiles. Bud's eyes followed her constantly and I noticed that when she left our group Mike watched her in a lazy fashion, his eyes half-closed as if he didn't want me to know he was looking at her. Maybe he merely liked to see her curving legs and rounded body. All the other boys did, and I admitted grudgingly to myself that she was the best-looking girl at the lake. Beside her, I felt positively drab.

When Jill came back from one of her treks to other people, she put her hand lightly on Mike's shoulder as she passed him. "You have one elegant set of muscles, Mike Maxwell," she purred, and took a seat by Bud.

Her tone made me sick. After all, Mike wasn't her date and she'd sounded overly possessive in her simpering way. I thought Mike would see through such an obvious effort to draw his attention to her, since she was trying boldly to butter him up, but he continued to grin as if the two of them shared a secret. That hurt me, too. He wasn't looking at me with that kind of dreamy expression and I wondered what memories of their long-ago dates made them exchange such glowing glances.

After a time she and Bud went to the concession stand for food and Mike announced that he thought he'd take a swim. "Coming, Christy?" he asked.

I didn't budge from my beach towel. "I don't think so. The lake has to be polluted with so many people in it. This isn't my thing."

"You were the one who wanted to go someplace today. Remember? I tried to tell you. If you think this is a mob, I'll bet there are twice as many at the State Park."

"Mike" — I lowered my voice — "I wish we'd come in your car. Then we could leave. Do you mind suggesting it to Bud and Jill?"

I knew at once I'd made him mad. The pulse in his temple started to throb and he glared at me as if he didn't think he'd heard correctly. "What's wrong with you today?" he barked. "We haven't been here two hours."

"Nothing's wrong, Mike. I simply said I'd like to go and you're making a federal case out of it."

"Yeah. Don't blame me, Christy. You're the one sulking, not me."

"I am not sulking!"

"Back at your house you acted awfully uptight when we were doing that puzzle, and in the car coming out here you clammed up and didn't say a word." His voice was thick with anger even though he was speaking in an undertone. "Now you want to go home and that's practically the only remark you've made to anybody. For your information, Bud and I paid extra admission at the gate because it's a holiday and the entrance fees are always double then, and I, for one, intend to get my money's worth and I think Bud does, too! So if you're hell-bent on being a party pooper, Christy, have yourself a ball! But I'm not going to let you spoil my fun, although you're sure giving it a big try!"

My mouth dropped open. Mike ran to the lake, leaping over people sprawled full-length on the ground and wading out past the little children and old ladies sitting at the water's edge, until he was waist deep and could swim. A lump as big as a tangerine was lodged in my throat. Mike and I had never had a quarrel and he'd never spoken to me in such a cross, critical way. I didn't think I'd been uptight when we were at my house and the reason I hadn't talked in the car — one of the reasons — was because it was hard to get a word in with Jill rattling on and on.

Mike's anger had to be because we were with Jill. It had to be her fault, I decided. The hurt from all of it churned deep inside me and my eyes blurred like they always did if they were filling with tears. *I won't cry*, I told myself over and over, blinking hard, and I didn't cry, thankful for the dark glasses which sheltered my eyes from other people as well as from the sun.

Far out in the lake, the top of Mike's head was a tiny speck as he cut through the water with hard, swift strokes, swimming so fast he could have been trying to set a record. Jill and Bud returned with a mammoth, red-paper cone of hot popcorn, offering some to me but I said no. I continued to watch the dim figure in the water, and when Jill asked where Mike had gone, I gestured in the direction of the lake.

"I don't see him. Oh, is that Mike way out there? He's awfully far from shore."

She sounded concerned and I didn't want her to be solicitous about him. That was my privilege because he was dating me now and what he did wasn't her business. I was frightened, though. The lake had to be very, very deep where Mike was and if he got a cramp or had any kind of trouble, it might be too late to save him by the time the life guard arrived.

Jill held her hand up to shade her eyes from the reflection of the sun on the water as she continued to watch, and each of us let out a long breath when Mike finally turned and started to swim toward land. Apparently realizing she and I were apprehensive, Bud gave a big guffaw of laughter, and Jill, who'd held the paper cone without eating popcorn while she watched Mike, began to nibble.

I knew I was terribly jealous of Jill. I also

knew all at once how Mike had felt when he thought there was something between Vince and me, and as much as I hated to think about it, I was jealous of Jill's beauty, her figure, her personality, her ability to charm boys. Maybe I wouldn't have felt so strongly about her if she hadn't once been Mike's girl, and the terrifying truth was that my jealousy wasn't harming her one bit, but it was ripping me wide open.

On the way back to town that night Jill and Bud got into an argument. It began around eight o'clock, when we were walking to his car, all of us disgruntled and hungry because the concession stand had run out of food, and the boys, who'd gone there to get hot dogs for our supper, returned empty-handed.

I'd been ready to leave ever since we arrived and now the others agreed there was no reason to stay at the lake any longer. Mike and I were pretending we hadn't exchanged angry words, neither of us referring to it and both of us studiedly polite. As the sun went down the mosquitoes came out and we slapped at our legs while we gathered up the damp towels and trudged down the road to Bud's car. Fighting the mob at the bath house a second time was unthinkable and I pulled my shorts and shirt on over my swim suit. Jill did the same.

We were scarcely past the entrance when a car came by and slowed. There were six boys in that automobile and the driver yelled,

"Have you heard from Vince, Jill?" His voice seemed familiar although in the semi-darkness I didn't recognize him.

"Vince is in Ohio," she answered. " 'Nuff said. When something's over, it's o-v-e-r." She spelled the word out.

"So that means you're available, huh? I'll phone you sometime."

"Pete, you be sure to do that," she said gaily as the car raced off.

The four of us continued in silence, walking single file along the edge of the road with Bud in front, then Jill. I came next and Mike was last. Cars went by and a short distance further along we heard a roaring noise behind us, which grew louder and louder in intensity, accompanied by long beams of light. I realized motorcycles were coming and didn't expect them to stop although two did, the guy in front pushing his helmet visor off his face as he said, "Hey, Jill Rogers! Want a lift to wherever you're going?"

I knew him slightly. Carl Browning attended Greenview High. He was a tall boy who'd been on the school basketball team. I couldn't tell about the identity of his companion who didn't remove his visor or speak. Both Bud and Mike knew Carl although neither of them said a word.

The motorcycles chugged and sputtered as Jill left us and walked into the middle of the road to Carl. "Oh, sure," she laughed. "I'd love a ride." Carl tossed her his spare helmet and I couldn't believe what I was seeing when she put it on and buckled the strap under her chin before climbing on the seat behind him.

"Now, hold it!" Bud said furiously. "I thought you were with me tonight, Jill!"

"I am, Bud." She wrapped her arms around Carl's waist. "Carl's only going to take me to where you parked your car. You know I never have been much of a walker."

The two motorcycles took off with a deafening *vroooooom*! which sent road dust into my mouth and eyes. It was too dark for me to get a good look at Mike's face but there was no mistaking Bud's reaction. He was snorting, muttering to himself as he walked ahead of us, and finally he sprinted off into the night.

"The perfect ending of a not-so-perfect day," I murmured sarcastically. To my amazement, Mike laughed, although there wasn't a great deal of mirth in the sound.

I honestly thought Jill had gone on to Greenview with Carl but when Mike and I reached the car Bud was behind the wheel, gunning the engine, and Jill sat so far to the other side of the front seat she was almost falling out of the door. Carl and his motorcycle weren't to be seen, and Bud scarcely gave us a chance to get in the back before he shot the car out into the road with such swiftness that I was thrown against Mike. Mama's admonition came back to me, how she'd said the Fourth was one of the worst times of year for traffic accidents. If we had a wreck, it would be Bud's fault for driving like a maniac.

"Cool it, Bud!" Mike said roughly. "Are

you trying to kill us or just bucking to be arrested for recklessness?"

Bud didn't reply but he eased up on the accelerator and I searched my brain for something to say, not coming up with any remark which seemed appropriate. I guess each of us was mad, but for different reasons. We covered five or six miles when Mike said, "If it's all right with you two, Christy and I'd rather not stop for something to eat. You can drop us at her house and we'll — "

"Okay, okay," Bud grunted without waiting for Mike to finish.

Jill, her head turned toward the window with her profile showing, tilted her chin up. As much as she usually chattered and giggled, I was surprised at her ability to keep so quiet for such a long time.

My hill seemed lovely and peaceful after the hubbub at the lake and the tension in Bud's car. I was glad to get my feet on the ground and the tires squealed as Bud zoomed down the drive.

"I hope he makes it home in one piece," Mike said as much to himself as to me.

"Do you suppose he and Jill will argue now that they don't have us for an audience, or just go their separate ways?" I asked.

"I don't know or care. Right now I'm a heck of a lot more interested in eating than in talking about what they'll do, but I figured if I didn't get away from them I'd go nuts. We can grab a hamburger or pizza or whatever you want."

The one thing I didn't want was to get

back on the highway or fight the mob at a drive-in. Staying at my house in the cool quiet seemed much nicer.

"Mike, we probably don't have any cooked food in the house but we always have bacon and eggs in the refrigerator, and I can fix that for us if you like. In case you're interested, I make marvelous cinnamon toast."

"Sounds super. I — "

"Christy, is that you?" Mama called from the window and Dad loomed up behind her. Mike and I were still in the yard where Bud had put us out. "Thank you for coming early, dear," she said. "Did you have a good time?"

I managed a yes, hoping she wouldn't ask for details about the trip to Coburn's Lake, and Dad's voice rang out with a question. "Mike, was that you burning rubber on the drive?"

"No, sir. I left my car here when we went to the lake. Tires are too expensive for me to mutilate one like that."

I reflected quietly that it was kind of Mike not to mention Bud's name, not to clear himself by incriminating someone else, but being thoughtful came naturally to Mike most of the time. It wasn't hard to guess that the day had been a disappointment to him just as it was to me, and the fact that my frustration and anger were fading at last left me embarrassed because I'd contributed my share to the day's unpleasantness.

Tomorrow I'd apologize to Mama for the breakfast argument, I decided. As for Mike, I waited until we finished our final bites of food to tell him I realized I'd been hard to get along with all day. When I said it we were still at the kitchen table with a fat yellow candle burning between us, the wax dripping in little globs onto the bottom of the glass holder. Our bacon, eggs, and cinnamon toast had been delicious.

"For a change I'm apologizing to you." I ducked my head slightly.

"Christy, I was about to tell you I hope you can forgive and forget the stuff I said this afternoon at the lake. I was — well, I don't have much of an excuse."

"I've already forgotten. There wasn't anything to forgive."

It was the easiest thing in the world for us to smile at each other. The tenderness shone in his eyes, and we reached our hands across the table, twining our fingers together.

"Let's get the dishes done in a hurry so we can go outside," he said softly.

Slipping one hand from his grasp, I traced the shape of his mouth with my forefinger. "Why don't we stack the dishes, Mike? I'll wash them in the morning."

He smiled and blew out the candle, each of us picking up a plate and iced-tea glass, setting them down in the sink very carefully so they wouldn't clatter. It seemed important not to mar the moment with unnecessary noise and we eased the screen door shut behind us and stepped out into the flower-scented darkness. The stars were sparkling their brightest and the air was fresh and clean against my cheeks. Mike's arm felt just right around my shoulders and we were so eager to kiss we didn't wait until we reached the rock bench.

There was a footnote to the events of the Fourth of July. On the night of the fifth when Mike and I again were in the yard he told me he'd seen Bud late in the afternoon and that the Bud-Jill romance was over.

"For keeps, I guess. Christy, he's bound to realize she was giving him the shabbiest sort of treatment when she got on the motorcycle with Carl, but he's going to have a rough adjustment, just the same. He's loved Jill all his life."

"How could he when she hadn't been nice to him, unless she wanted a date on the spur of the moment?"

"I've been thinking about that all day." Mike ran his fingers through his hair and locked his hands at the back of his head. "Jill can be great when she wants to be. Really great. I guess the fact that Bud's so darned ugly and she's so beautiful could be a factor. He knows she has something in the way of looks he can never have. But the crazy part is that Bud's ugly on the outside and beautiful inside, and Jill — well, it's not like that with her. Usually she thinks about herself before she thinks about other people."

We were silent a few minutes. "What about Sharon?" I asked.

"She wasn't mentioned. I can't believe Bud stood her up. Jill has stood him up so often he wouldn't do that to somebody else.

Maybe he phoned her to cancel their date, or maybe she's found a guy in Richmond at her school."

"Mike, did you know Bud would be with Jill yesterday?"

"I didn't. I swear it. You could have knocked me over with a feather when I saw Jill in the car." He sucked his breath in and gave a low chuckle. "Want to know something wild, Christy? Last spring when Jill had a few dates with Bud during one of the times she and Vince were at each other's throats, I told Bud I'd bet him a dollar that before the middle of July Vince and Jill would be finished and that if he — Bud — was dating her again he'd wish he wasn't. Turns out I was right, wasn't I? Guess I'll have to collect that buck when I get around to it."

The thought of boys betting money on anything involving a girl was rankling. "Did you also make a bet on how long you'd be dating me?" I asked stiffly.

"No, Christy! You know better. Look — " He put his hand under my chin and gently lifted my face to his, leaning forward to kiss me on the mouth. "I hope you and I never stop caring about each other."

Chapter

· 18 ·

The trip to Indiana was something to be tolerated, not relished, and I guess going anyplace with that negative attitude meant I wouldn't have a whiz-bang time. In contrast, Mama was excited. She referred to those two weeks in Indiana as "going home," but I'd noticed in the past summers she always seemed more satisfied after Dad arrived, and by the time we told Aunt Doris good-bye and came back to wherever we were living, she was content to pick up her day-to-day life once more. She must feel about Dad as I did about Mike, I mused.

Since Greenview was too small a community for air service, Dad drove us ninety miles to Roanoke to catch a plane west. During the ride Mama commented that as soon as we returned to Virginia she and I ought to go to Roanoke for the day to shop. "Last autumn we didn't add to your school wardrobe at all, and this winter in the rush of moving and getting settled here, it never got done," she said. "Besides, I expect you've reached your full height now, Christy."

I hoped I'd grown as much as I would. At five feet, seven inches, I was taller than some of the boys at school and was thankful Mike was more than six feet. Height seemed to run in his family as both his father and his uncle Eb were tall men.

The plane cruised along at such a high altitude I could only see puffs of white clouds and not the earth when I looked out of the window, and my mind was more on Mike than school clothes or the trip. He and I had slipped back into our comfortable closeness during the week since the Fourth. There were drives to Sonny's for ice cream and we'd seen a movie, but the best times were the delicious moments on the rock bench. "Our spot," we called it, and laughed about the hardness of the seat which didn't seem the least bit important when our arms were around each other.

Betsy would be coming home from Maryland in a few days, and we'd seen Gordon once since the Fourth, and Bud twice, all of it rather casual, although Bud had little to say. I didn't believe he was over the hurt of Jill's actions and I wondered what she was doing with herself but I kept quiet about those matters. Saying Jill's name left a bitter taste on my tongue and I didn't want to spoil the short time Mike and I had together before I went away by discussing her. She wouldn't be lonely, not the way she attracted boys. If she didn't have a date, she'd go out and find one, the way she must have contacted Bud.

On our final evening Mike kissed me warmly. "I wish I didn't have to go to Indiana," I murmured for the hundredth time, my head buried in the hollow of his shoulder. "Will you write me, Mike?"

"You know I'm not much of a letter writer."

"You wouldn't have to exert yourself much just to write a postcard." I brought out a slip of paper and put it in the pocket of his jeans, telling him it had Aunt Doris' address.

He laughed and kissed the tip of my nose. "Are you going to write me, Christy?"

"Do you want me to?"

"You bet."

"Then I will. I promise."

"Even if I don't get around to putting words on paper for you, I'll miss you," he whispered. "I'll think about you every minute."

Indiana was flat and sticky hot, with the land parched from a month of intense heat without any rain. Aunt Doris, who was waiting at the airport for us, had been a gray-haired lady the previous summer and now her hair was a soft, light brown.

"I'm a champagne blond, according to my

beauty operator," she said and laughed, patting her curls self-consciously when we told her we thought the new color was becoming.

Her husband had been dead so long I could barely remember him and none of her children lived at home at the present. She slept downstairs while Mama and I were in separate rooms on the second floor of the hundred-year-old house with its quaint dormers and a stained-glass window on the stair landing.

There were certain rituals connected with our annual trips to Indiana. Mama and I paid brief calls on relatives and made a point of going to see Miss Annie Comstock who had been both of my parents' third-grade teacher and was now an invalid. We always went to services at the church Mama attended as a little girl and there was at least one lunch at the Hoosierland Tea Room, which was managed by a distant cousin.

On the night after Dad arrived, Aunt Doris invited several people in for coffee and cake which meant I answered polite questions about my school, just as I'd done in the past about other schools. Lying in bed afterward, I thought about what I'd write Mike. I'd already written him a long letter and sent a silly post card which had a picture of a man milking a cow on it, but I hadn't received any mail from him and I'd scarcely let Dad get out of the car before asking if he'd seen Mike.

"No, I haven't, Christy. I stopped at the

service station twice this past week but Mike wasn't there either time." Dad grinned and winked at me. "A good looking young chap like Mike Maxwell probably was out with a girl."

I knew my father was teasing me but that kind of talk hurt. "Bryan, don't," Mama said quickly and I could have hugged her for it.

"As best I can remember," Dad went on, serious now as if he realized his attempt at fun was upsetting, "the tow truck wasn't where it's usually parked at the service station. Mike must have been out on a service call."

I hoped that's the way it was, hoped it so much I felt quivery inside, and because I was afraid I'd give my feelings away if we continued to talk about Mike, I picked up a magazine and pretended to be reading.

There was only one out-of-the-ordinary event during the stay in Indiana and it wasn't something I intended discussing in my letters to Mike. Aunt Doris insisted on arranging a date for me with a boy whose mother was one of her friends.

"Thanks, but I'd rather not. I have a boy friend at home," I told her the first time she brought up the subject, thinking how ironic it was that I no longer cared about a blind date. The previous year when Aunt Doris called me a "late bloomer," but didn't offer to introduce me to any boys, I'd have been ecstatic at the thought of meeting people.

The following day she mentioned the date

again and I protested again, which didn't phase her at all. "But surely you want to go with other boys, Christy." Her voice showed her irritation. "Hubert will be over at eight tonight. Hubert Evans. He's about your age and it's already arranged and I know you'll like him. His mother is a charming person."

All my willpower was needed not to tell her he could have the most marvelous mother in the world and still be a clod himself. It didn't matter to me if my blind date was the Prince of Wales, I didn't want anybody but Mike.

"Aunt Doris, I don't — "

"Christy!" Mama interrupted me in her obey-and-hush voice.

I saw the warning look in her eyes because she didn't want any friction but it didn't stop me from one final effort. "I'm not inter-ested in a date." I pronounced each word clearly and I knew I might as well have spoken to one of the potted ferns in the wicker stand on Aunt Doris' porch. As my aunt said, the evening was already arranged.

Hubert Evans was as disinterested in me as I was in him, and I had the feeling his mothered ordered him to keep the date just as my aunt and my mother were ordering me. We went to the movies, had Cokes afterward, and talked about his school and mine, then about sports, and I was relieved that he didn't suggest another date.

"How did you and Hubert get along?" Aunt Doris asked at breakfast the next morning. "Isn't he nice? I told you his mother is my dearest friend."

I agreed he was nice and assured her I'd had a good time, not knowing what I'd say if she wanted to know how soon I was seeing Hubert again. Fortunately, the question didn't come.

Chapter

· 19 ·

The ride back to Virginia seemed extraordinarily long, or maybe it dragged because I was anxious to be with Mike. The interstate highways bypassed towns, and the road had an uninteresting sameness with woods and fields sliding out of view in a monotous procession. Dad did most of the driving although Mama and I helped too.

We left northern Indiana after lunch Saturday and expected to be in Greenview early Sunday afternoon, stopping for the night at a motel. This was Mama's suggestion as she felt it would be less tiring for all of us than driving straight through in one very long day as Dad had done when he came west. He had to go to work Monday after we returned, so splitting the trip would give him Sunday afternoon to unwind, and Mama added that it would allow us to unpack and air the house before bedtime. I knew she was eager to see her garden, and the earlier in the day we arrived, the better it suited me. I'd written Mike that I'd call him just as soon as we were in the house.

Nothing went right Sunday. We checked out of the motel Sunday morning to discover we had a flat tire, and the second delay came a couple of hours later when Mama was driving and the automobile slowed even though she was pressing on the gas pedal. She managed to coast off the pavement to the shoulder, with a dead engine that refused to start again. Dad, his head under the hood while he checked various parts of the motor, commented that he didn't know if the problem was in the fuel pump or the carburetor but that Sunday morning was the devil of a time to try to locate a mechanic when we were ten miles from nowhere.

Several cars whizzed by us without stopping and after almost an hour a highway patrolman come, radioing for a tow truck which took us to a garage at a country crossroads. As Dad suspected, the trouble was with the carburetor. It was an additional three hours before the repairs were made and we were on our way once more.

There was nowhere for Mama and me to wait except on a wobbly bench pushed against the building and it was fearfully hot, the sun blazing down and the air motionless. Every now and then one of us would get up and walk around a little and I knew she had to be as uncomfortable as I was, but she didn't fidget while I found it hard to sit still. My clothes were stuck to my body with perspiration and my hair, which I'd shampooed just before leaving Aunt Doris' house, felt matted against my scalp. Looking at my watch was a mistake as it made me realize how slowly time was passing.

Once we were on the road again the car air conditoner sent out a stream of coolness and I'd have liked to go all the way to Greenview without stopping except to buy gas, but around four in the afternoon Dad and Mama wanted a meal. Our lunch had consisted of stale peanut butter and cracker sandwiches and lukewarm orange soda from a malfunctioning vending machine at the garage, and I had to admit I was hungry, although the desire to see Mike was stronger than any yearning for food.

It was that dim, misty time between twilight and full darkness when Dad turned from the highway into our drive. The mountains loomed dark blue in the distance against a paler blue-gray sky and our house was a tall white sentinel on top of the hill. Suddenly I realized that this house with all the crazy windows was home to me. I was where I belonged and I felt good seeing it, felt good knowing I was there. Everything on our hill was silent and peaceful and blessedly cool, the way home should be after a long, hot, trying day.

"Susan, think you can wait for morning to get out in the garden?" Dad asked Mama. "While you were gone I told the Saylors to help themselves to vegetables and flowers but I expect you'll still have more than we can use. Your tomato crop is going to surpass the green peas."

Mama said something to him which I didn't hear, their voices fading as I ran indoors to the phone. When I dialed Mike's house his mother answered. "It's Christy Jamison, Mrs. Maxwell," I said, my voice breathless with excitement. "May I speak to Mike?"

"He's not here, Christy."

She sounded almost curt. I wondered if she had guests or if I'd interrupted one of her favorite TV programs. "Will you tell him I called?" I asked and had a better thought. "Do you know how I can reach him right now? I've been out of town and just came home."

"He didn't say where he was going, Christy. Try Jill Rogers. Jill ought to know where he is if anybody does."

I'd been standing up and I sat down quickly. I hope I told her good-bye but wasn't sure and a terrible throbbing pain began inside of me. Mike and Jill . . . I'd been away two weeks and I hadn't heard from him. He must have been seeing a lot of Jill if his own mother knew Jill Rogers could locate him. *Don't let it be . . . don't let it be . . . don't let it be,* I said silently and the words were a prayer.

In the Monday morning sunshine my mother's garden showed it had been neglected for two weeks. Dead flowers drooped on dry stalks which should have been watered or cut, and small green weeds had sprung up between the rows of plants. While we were away the marigolds had come into full bloom, the fat orange and yellow blossoms as round as saucers. The asters were just showing color when we left and now they were a shaggy profusion of blues, lavenders and every shade of pink.

"Cut some flowers for the house, Christy," Mama said. "Just stick them in a bucket of water for now and you can arrange them in vases later. The first thing we need to do is pick all the ripe vegetables. I'm not in the mood to can tomatoes but I expect I'll have to do it this afternoon to save them since they're so ripe. Your daddy was right when he said we'd have a bumper crop."

Red tomatoes of all sizes hung heavily on the staked plants, and next to them were the turnips and squash. A patch of broccoli was ready to be cut and the cucumber vines were out of control, spreading in every direction.

I worked like a robot, doing what Mama told me to do, bending over the plants or kneeling in the soft black earth to pull up weeds. The day became warmer as the sun moved higher but there was none of the suffocating heat we'd experienced the previous day, when we were waiting for the carburetor to be repaired. Our hill had a breeze and some white butterflies flitted around us, hovering over the flowers.

About eleven o'clock that morning I

couldn't stand it any longer. "Mama, if you can spare me a little while and if I can use your car, I'd like to go into town," I said and straightened up, brushing dirt from my legs.

She stopped picking tomatoes and looked at me. "It isn't smart for a girl to chase after a boy, Christy. I don't know what's happened to Mike, but I think you ought to wait and let him come to you. I don't like to think about your going down to the service station and maybe getting involved in a scene. That's a very public place."

With her uncanny ability to read my thoughts she knew what I was going to do. The night before she'd found me sitting in the den in the dark after my conversation with Mrs. Maxwell, and I'd said only that Mike wasn't at home but his mother would give him a message. I waited until bedtime before giving up hope, praying silently he would phone, and he hadn't. Even after Dad and Mama were in their room and I was in mine with the hall door closed and the lights out, I sat on the window seat, hoping I'd see the headlights of Mike's car coming up the hill.

It took me a long time to go to sleep and I woke early Monday. Going through the motions of breakfast was an ordeal and I didn't fool my parents, who were decent enough not to mention my not eating. At first I thought as Mama did that I should wait until Mike got in touch with me. The entire time she and I were in the garden Monday morning

I listened for the sound of the telephone, listened so hard my ears ached.

By eleven o'clock I couldn't torture myself any longer by waiting. I had to know, and if Mike wouldn't come to me, I had to go to him.

"Christy." Mama cleared her throat as if she wasn't sure of what to say. "These things happen. You're welcome to use my car, but if you insist on going into town to see Mike, tell yourself in advance you're going to stay calm no matter what happens."

I didn't know if I'd ever feel calm again, but I nodded to her. Going upstairs, I showered and put on a wrap-around blue denim skirt and a fresh white cotton blouse. Lipstick put a faint rosy color on my lips but it didn't do much for the somberness in my eyes.

Mike was handing change to a customer when I drove up. *"Christy!"* he gasped and came running to the car, his eyes widening in amazement. "When did you get home?"

He hadn't known it. I was positive of that. Nobody could fake that sort of surprise.

"Last night," I said and there was a prickly sensation on my tongue as if I'd bitten into a fresh peach and had the fuzz in my mouth. "I phoned you and your mother said she'd tell you."

"Mom never said a word! What time did you call?"

"Around eight-thirty." My hands were clasped tightly together in my lap to stop them from trembling. "I asked her where you were so I could get in touch with you and she told me to call Jill Rogers."

"What th — Look, Christy, I wasn't at Jill's! I went to the movies last night with Gordon and Betsy. The three of us. Did you think . . . ?"

He knew what I thought, and I knew I'd been wrong. But I had to know the rest of it.

"Mike, you didn't write. Didn't you get the mail I sent you?"

"I lost that piece of paper with your aunt's address. I must have left it in the pocket of my jeans and it went through the washing machine and it was just a ball of pulp when I discovered it. But I haven't been in town, Christy. My brother came unexpectedly. Jack, the one who works for a building contractor in Pennsylvania. He was on the way to Atlanta to a convention and asked if I'd like to go along just for the trip. Uncle Eb gave me the time off and Jack had several days of vacation time so we came home by way of the Carolina coast and stopped at some beaches. I didn't get back to Greenview until Saturday noon."

I wanted to touch him, to reach out my hands and touch his hands and his face, only I didn't do anything except sit there and smile.

"Christy, it's almost noon," he said, lowering his voice. "I get an hour for lunch and we're not busy so I can go now. Want to come with me? We'll grab something at a drive-in."

"I'd like that. But first I have to call home. Mama thought I'd only be gone a few minutes."

While I went to the pay phone at the side of the service station he spoke to his uncle, and when my mother answered I burst out with, "I'm having lunch with Mike! I'll be home after a while!"

"Is everything all right, dear?"

"Everything's wonderful! Just plain wonderful!"

I got into Mike's car, sitting so close to him our legs touched, and as soon as we were away from the station he put one arm around my shoulders and pulled me even closer. He drove past Sonny's and past two drive-ins, turning off the highway just after the town limits sign and going down a narrow unpaved lane. When he braked we were in a grove of old oaks with two chimneys standing as stark evidence that once a house stood on that spot.

Tree branches bent low and the sun made dappled shadows around us. Honeysuckle vines were everywhere, the yellow and white flowers almost too sweet, and clear water in a small stream trickled over some smooth, round rocks. It was a lovely, private place, the perfect place for kisses on a summer day, and Mike's mouth was as warm and delicious as I remembered.

Chapter

· 20 ·

My mother and I were in a happy-go-lucky mood as we started to Roanoke to shop on a sun-washed August morning. I couldn't believe school would be starting in three weeks or that I'd be a senior. Mike would be a senior, too, of course. Just thinking his name made me smile and gave me a nice, tingling feeling inside.

I drove the first forty of the ninety miles from Greenview to Roanoke, pulling up at a highway restaurant Mike had recommended. "It serves the best homemade pecan buns you ever ate," he'd said, and Mama and I decided he was right. We even bought a bag of them to take back to him and we lingered at the restaurant counter, sitting on high stools as we talked about the clothes I needed. Hurrying wasn't necessary, as we'd made such an early start from home there was time to kill unless we wanted to reach Roanoke before the stores were open.

Mama took the wheel when we started out again. She commented on how well-engineered the four-lane highway was, the road flat although the terrain on either side was hilly with the blue mountains in the distance.

"Look at that!" she gasped, her eyes on the rear view mirror. "Oh, no — "

I turned quickly to peer out of the back window and saw two cars coming behind us, obviously racing. They were side by side and going terribly fast.

Mama began slowing down and got as far to the right side of the road as possible. The first car zoomed by us but the second slammed into our car and I heard the horrible crunch of metal on metal and felt our automobile flying through the air half on its side with me doubled up against the door and Mama shoved on top of me so that I couldn't breathe, and everything whirling and the mountains and the ground coming closer and closer — until there was nothing.

The first thing I saw when I opened my eyes was a green ceiling. All our ceilings at home were white and I thought I must be in a motel but I couldn't remember going to one ... couldn't remember anything for a minute. I knew I was lying down and I tried to turn and couldn't because of the jabbing pain in my forehead when I moved. Then I tried to reach out and my left arm wouldn't budge.

"Christy." It was Dad's voice.

My eyes began to focus and he was standing beside the bed with Mama sitting in a big chair next to him. She got up and stood beside him and she looked strange, her skin chalky and her lips quivering. There was a dark yellowish-purple bruise on her cheek and her mouth seemed swollen.

"You're all right, Christy," Dad said. "So is your mother. You were in an accident on the way to Roanoke this morning but you're all right. Do you understand?"

"I — I think so." It was coming back to me. The two cars racing behind us, the brutal splintering noise when one of those cars hit us, the frightening sensation of falling . . . and falling . . .

"Mama?" I said, my panic showing in my voice.

"I'm here, Christy." She picked up my right hand.

"Are you hurt, Mama?"

"Not much, dear. Some bruises and a small cut or two."

"How much am I hurt?"

Above the bed I saw her look at Dad. "I'll be truthful with you, Christy. You have a mild concussion but the doctors don't think it's anything to be concerned about although you probably have a headache. They want to keep you here in the hospital overnight as a precaution. Your left arm is broken. If it feels heavy, that's because it's been put in a cast."

"Hospital? What hospital?"

"If you had to be in an accident," Dad smiled, "you picked the best location. There was a county hospital just a mile away, and you're about an hour from home. Fifty miles, more or less."

I asked what time it was and Dad said ten minutes to two in the afternoon, and then I asked about the accident. Neither of the speeding cars stopped after we were sideswiped and knocked off the road down into a ravine, but a truck driver did, Mama said. He was behind us and was almost hit by the cars as they dashed by him. He saw our accident and summoned the police and an ambulance with his CB radio and waited until help arrived.

A doctor came into the hospital room and put his fingers on my pulse telling me he was glad I was awake and asking how I felt. I mentioned the headache and the blond nurse with him went out and returned to give me a shot and the pain went away. I dozed a little and when I woke up again the room was shadowy.

"Christy, how do you feel?" Dad leaned over me.

"Better. My head isn't throbbing now."

"That's good. I've been trying to persuade your mother to go home but she wanted to stay here until you were fully conscious, and you are now. She's had a long, rough day, though, and a bad shock, and if you'll be all right without us for a couple of hours, I'm going to drive her home and put her to bed and then I'll come back to see about you."

"I don't need you to come back tonight, Dad," I whispered. "You stay with Mama. There are nurses and doctors here to take care of me and I can ring the bell if I need anything, but Mama needs somebody to look after her."

"Are you sure you don't mind?"

"I'm sure," I said. Dad kissed me very carefully on the cheek and Mama did the same. She was still pale and trembly.

The room seemed very quiet when they were gone and I tried to choke back the feeling of loneliness. Muted noises came from the corridor, a wheeled cart going by . . . the click of ice cubes in a metal pitcher, although the nurse carrying the pitcher walked silently. I turned my head away from the open door to look at the other side of the room where a bed was made up, waiting for the next patient, the counterpane very white.

The nurse who brought my supper tray elevated my head slightly and said if I couldn't feed myself she'd help me. "Give it a try," she smiled. "I'll check on you in a few minutes."

I hadn't thought about being hungry which was fortunate since the tray only contained a bowl of chicken soup and a small dish of custard. At least it's my left arm that's broken and not my right, I reminded myself. The soup was hot to my throat and it seemed to jar my face to chew even the small cubes of chicken, so I ate the liquid and the custard, letting them sit on my tongue and slide slowly down.

"Good girl," the nurse said when she came back. She took the tray and lowered the bed so that I was lying flat once more. Moving my head no longer caused stabs of violent pain, although I couldn't turn quickly. I closed my eyes, not sleeping but just being still.

"Christy . . ." It was Mike.

I don't know why I should have cried at the sight of him, but I did, not wild sobs but quiet little ones with tears gathering in the corners of my eyes. It frightened him. I could see the consternation in his eyes and he held my right hand between both of his and begged, "Please don't, Christy. Don't cry. Do you want me to go find a nurse? Please don't cry."

"T-They're h-happy tears. I'm h-happy because you're h-here."

"Does it hurt much?"

"Seeing you makes everything better." It was true.

"When I found out about the wreck I thought I'd die. Christy, I guess I would have if they hadn't let me in to see you. Your dad phoned the hospital and got permission for me to come, which is the only reason I was allowed in your room."

"How did you find out about the accident?"

"Your dad and mother stopped at the station late this afternoon. I gathered Mr. Jamison wanted to take her straight to the house but she insisted they stop because she

248

was afraid if I left work they couldn't get in touch with me immediately in case I wanted to come to the hospital. I'm glad they did. I came straight on."

"I'm glad, too," I whispered.

We didn't talk much after that. Somehow, we didn't need words to communicate and Mike held my good hand, every few minutes lifting it to his mouth and kissing my fingers. I tried to smile at him so he wouldn't worry about me but my mouth felt twisted and the smile couldn't have looked right.

About an hour later a nurse came to the door of the room and told Mike to leave. "Miss Jamison needs her rest," the nurse said. She was one I hadn't seen before, older than the others with very gray hair and wearing a uniform starched so heavily it made a crinkling sound when she moved.

Mike got to his feet without letting go of my right hand. "Couldn't I wait just a little longer?" he asked. "It's early. Just twenty-five after eight."

"Visiting hours will be over in five minutes. You may as well go on now."

Mike's heart was in his eyes. "Please," he said softly to the nurse. "Christy and I are — well, she's my girl and — "

I saw the nurse shake her head and she disappeared into the hall, and Mike bent over me and kissed me tenderly on the mouth. "I'll be back to see you tomorrow," he whispered. "Thank God you'll be okay. I couldn't bear it if you weren't."

"Did you mean what you said, Mike? About — about my being your girl?"

His eyebrows lifted in astonishment. "Sure. Why wouldn't I mean it? Didn't you know?"

Yes, I knew. Almost knew. But I needed to hear the words, needed to hear him speak them.

He stooped to kiss me again, the pressure of his lips hard enough to make my bruised mouth ache, but I didn't mind. It was a good pain, a wonderful pain.

"Don't you worry about anything, Christy. Like I told that nurse, you're my girl and that means no matter what."

The elderly nurse returned, standing in the doorway with her hands at her sides, the skirt of her uniform like a white bell around her legs as she waited to see Mike go. He gave my good hand a gentle squeeze and walked past her into the hall, his footsteps as silent as the nurse's.

Mike's girl. I closed my eyes and repeated the phrase to myself. *Mike's girl.* It had a lovely sound.